PRAISE FOR TH
MURDER

Well, well, well this book makes for a rollercoaster of a ride. This book throws you around like washing in a tumble dryer. Throwing twist and turns at you until right at the very end. When the author is ready to lay out what has exactly been happening in this book and then boom everything makes sense. Wonderful.

- **Karen W**

A brilliantly twisted psychological thriller that kept me guessing right to the end. The plot was dark and complicated, yet easy to read. There were twists aplenty and secrets in abundance. The characters were well thought out and original, their background was revealed slowly, adding to the suspense. The descriptive writing transported me with ease to another country and culture. A really good read.

- **Sarah K**

I loved this book. The story was compelling and fairly easy to follow. The story although complex is enthralling and I didn't work out 'the whodunnit' until near the end. Definitely a good read. I will look out for more by this author.

- **Lenore S**

Ellie, Ellie, Ellie. What a ride. Behind Blue Eyes by Claire Duffy seductively draws you in and then tosses you around like a sock in a dryer. I loved how descriptive the setting was. It was easy to get completely lost in the twisted tale. I can't wait for the next in the series.

-**Rachelle S**

Copyright © 2022 by CS Duffy

All rights reserved.

No part of this book may be reproduced in any form or by any electronic or mechanical means, including information storage and retrieval systems, without written permission from the author, except for the use of brief quotations in a book review.

❋ Created with Vellum

ALL THE STARS ABOVE

STOCKHOLM MURDERS BOOK THREE

CS DUFFY

 BOOKS

1

'm not dead, she thought, and she wanted to scream.

The darkness was deep and thick and cloying and for a horrible moment she couldn't remember what her hands looked like. She held them up, peered desperately into nothing, but all she could see was unrelenting blackness. Could she even be sure anymore that she had hands? A tidal wave of panic rose up in her throat, threatened to choke her.

I'll believe it when I see it with my own two eyes, Pappa used to say, once upon a time. I don't believe in anything I can't see.

Her sister used to get so frustrated with him. She was the clever one. She understood physics and chemistry and how there are many things happening in the world that we can't see with our bare eyes. Pappa would shrug maddeningly and tell her that when she could show him a proton or a cell, he would believe it was there. Then he'd shake out his newspaper and continue to contentedly read while her sister glared.

Now she couldn't see anything with her own two eyes. Hadn't been able to for — hours? Days? No, it couldn't be that long. Could it? She didn't know any more. She couldn't believe anything anymore.

She would give anything to see her hands again.

She wanted light even more than she wanted escape. If she were given the choice right now, between the door being opened and she could go home but she would only ever see blackness again; and a chink of light but no release — she would take the latter.

The thought of the outside world was overwhelming. All those noises and people and questions. She couldn't handle it. She was safe here, alone in the quiet. Was this Stockholm Syndrome? Hadn't she read once that it wasn't real? That it was just misogynistic police dismissing the women's empathy for the man who had held them captive?

Did she have empathy? She didn't know. She didn't know anything. She just wanted to see her hands again.

2

It took a moment for the pain to come. The forest floor was soft and squelchy. Frosty dew seeped through my running tights. Tears sprang to my eyes as daggers shot up my leg.

My ankle smarted like nobody's business, jagged pain making me feel dizzy. I eyed the offending root which had sent me sprawling arse over tip, trying to decide if I was about to scream, puke, or cry. Or all three. *Christ*, it was sore. My whole body thrummed with it. I closed my eyes a moment, trying to breathe through the wave of wooziness.

Serves me right for becoming one of those fit keen people. The old me wouldn't have found herself in this predicament. She would have been tucked up in front of the telly, steaming pot of tea to hand, contentedly picking crisp crumbs off her boobs as drama kicked off on the latest reality trash. Like all right-minded people.

My gloveless hands stung with cold. A trickle of icy water had somehow made it under the collar of my thermal running top and was slithering unpleasantly down my spine. The mulched-up leaves beneath me were still sodden, but I noticed that the trees had stopped dripping melted snow. Uneasiness fluttered in my stomach. Dusk was gathering, driving the temperature back below zero. Easter was last week, but Sweden was horrifyingly slow at getting the memo it was spring.

It had been dull all day, the sun hidden behind a thick layer of white. Now the clouds had turned a deep purply-grey, and silence throbbed through the spindly trees. This forest was huge, spanning miles and miles up the coastline and quite far inland. Deer and moose roamed freely, and there had been great excitement in the village a few weeks earlier when the first wolf was spotted in decades. I was all for conservation but wouldn't have objected to wolf-less woods to run in, if the truth be told. Nerves prickled through me as I tried to remember how far I'd come.

I hadn't reached the church yet. I'd first spotted it whilst on a walk foraging for mushrooms months ago, and had been trying to work up the courage to clamber in and explore ever since. It was properly ancient, built from large, crumbling stones and I'd whiled away many a run lost in fantasies of stumbling across Viking loot buried under the altar. It was high on a hill, and while there wouldn't be much of a view today, I was sure that it would be possible to spot Finland across the Baltic Sea on a clear day.

My ankle was starting to swell ominously, bulging out my trainer in a wildly unwelcome manner. I couldn't be more than a couple of kilometres deep into the woods, I reminded myself. Three, at most. That was something. A quick glance at my phone showed it out of service, which was typical. For a tech-obsessed country, Sweden was remarkably stingy regarding mobile signal outside cities.

I reached for a nearby branch and unceremoniously hauled myself to my feet. Well, foot. Balancing on my good leg with the help of the branch, I tried putting weight on my wounded ankle, and —

With a strangled screech toppled right back onto the frosty ground.

'Fuckitalltoshit!' I roared into the silence. I was rewarded with an echo and an indignant squawk from a bird in the distance. A flutter of panic sprang to life in my stomach. I could almost feel the night's freeze creeping towards me, taunting me as it slowly tugged me into its lair.

'For heaven's sake,' I shouted sternly, out loud. My voice echoed back at me. 'Get a grip, Ellie.'

There was a solution to my predicament. There must be. Something simple. Something obvious. Something that would make me roll my eyes at myself and call myself a fanny just as soon as I thought of it. Which would be any moment now.

In the meantime, I gritted my teeth against waves of pain and reached for the branch. With a bit of effort, I yanked myself to my feet again. I waved my phone around a bit, in wild optimism that a bar of service would miraculously appear. Of course, even if it did, who exactly would I phone? Another trickle of dread unfurled itself in my guts. I firmly pushed it away.

No time for that now.

One problem at a time, I told myself, in a determinedly positive voice of the sort of character Julie Andrews might play. No use crying over spilt milk. Spit spot. A spoonful of sugar.

The second time I carefully tried my ankle, it proved to be a touch less dramatic. I could even walk, after a fashion, if I sort of clenched my foot to hold it steady. *That's better*, I thought as I inched forward. No problem. Slow and steady wins the race. If I was to have survived several run-ins with one of the most prolific serial killers in Sweden's history only to expire because of a twisted-bloody-ankle I was going to be mightily pissed off, I told myself firmly. I would write a strongly-worded letter of complaint. I would demand to see the manager.

My chuckle echoed in the stillness and I realised it was the first time I'd thought of Mia and had felt anything other than a tidal wave of horror. So that was progress.

Right before I froze to death.

Better late than never.

I was *not* going to freeze to death, I reminded myself in the Julie Andrews voice. I would not stand for such nonsense. I simply wouldn't *tolerate* hypothermia, thank you very much.

Moving was helping to warm me up ever so slightly. I sang a bit under my breath, a truly horrendous mashup between *My Favourite Things* and *A Spoonful of Sugar* that was as strangled as it was tuneless. I had just about got myself into a bit of a rhythm, barring the odd stumble and squeal of pain, when I saw him.

3

I froze, tiny nerves dancing on my spine. Dark had almost fallen and the man was barely a shadow, but his heavy footsteps on frosty bracken crashed through the silence. He was several metres ahead of me and just about to cross my path. If he glanced to his right he would see me.

I can't run, I thought, panic making my throat tight. I wanted to slip behind a tree but I was afraid of making a noise. I stood glued to the spot, grateful, for once, for the darkness. My heart thudded in my chest. He was striding purposefully. Angrily even, tension emanating off him in waves.

I never used to be this nervy. The treacherous thought fluttered through me and dread pooled in my stomach. But it was true. If I'd had a hairy canary every time I'd passed some random out an evening walk on Clapham Common, my teeth would have never stopped chattering. But I wasn't like that in those days. Once upon a time, I'd wandered through every inch of London at all hours. I never paid a blind bit of attention to who was around me. They didn't bother me, and I didn't bother them, which is just how it should be amongst city strangers. Now here I was, in a remote village a couple of hours north of Stockholm where nobody ever locked their doors, and I could practically hear the theme tune from *Psycho* screeching through my brain. I didn't want to be like this.

But something about his stride unnerved me. This wasn't an early evening stroll to blow away some cobwebs before dinner. He was a big guy, maybe not overly tall by Swedish standards, but he had the best part of a foot on me. His broad shoulders were taut. I couldn't quite make out his gloved hands in the gloom, but I was almost sure his fist was clenched.

He glanced in my direction. I shrank back —

Put too much weight on my bad ankle —

Clamped my hand over my mouth as my shout of pain resounded in my ears.

'Ellie?'

I looked up at the familiar voice and blinked like a weirdo as relief flooded through me.

'Axel!'

Oh, for heaven's sake. I was an idiot. Axel grinned as he jogged towards me, concern snapping in his eyes. He was one of those absurdly beautiful Swedes who has no idea he's absurdly beautiful because everyone he's ever met in his life is also an absurdly beautiful Swede. Tall, naturally, broad-shouldered, chiselled jaw, you get the picture. His wavy chestnut brown hair even flops in his eyes like a cartoon prince. I've wound him up about it more than once to which he stared, blankly with mild, polite confusion.

'What have you done to yourself? May I help?'

I nodded tightly, and in one smooth move, Axel leaned down and swooped me into his arms.

'Put me down!' I half-shouted, half-laughed, guilt and embarrassment and awkwardness prickling over me.

'But what? I thought you were hurt?' That sing-songy Scandinavian accent is stronger outside of Stockholm. He stared at me quizzically as I stared at the ground a moment, trying to catch my breath and hoping he couldn't see me blush in the darkness.

'I don't need to be carried,' I said a bit more sharply than I intended to. 'An arm to lean on will suffice, thank you so much.'

'I see.' He proffered a thick arm and I took it, leaning gratefully against him as we started to shuffle slowly along the path. My heart was still racing like nobody's business, which was just because of the exertion.

'I was in the shop today,' I blurted, trying to make this seem more like a normal conversation. 'Your mum was telling everyone the library is almost ready.' He made a *hmph* sound in his throat, which was Swedish for *don't remind me I have accomplished anything, it makes me very uncomfortable.*

Axel and I fell into conversation at the St Lucia parade last Christmas. His mum runs the local general shop, and she had organised a little stall selling glögg, which is Sweden's answer to mulled wine except there is a spirit in it and it blows your head off if you're not careful. I wasn't careful, because I assumed it was normal mulled wine, so I was pissed and giggly by the time the local junior school kids paraded up the village's only road, wearing crowns made from electric candles. Axel spotted me staggering off in the wrong direction and kindly guided me towards home. We ran into each other again a few weeks ago, and became occasional running buddies. I don't know him super well or anything, but it's nice to have company now and then.

'She will never forgive me for becoming an architect instead of taking over her store.'

'She sounded very proud to me,' I insisted loyally. In truth, Pernilla had pursed her lips and pointed out that she would have added a second storey, personally, but Axel knew best, of course. 'It's such an amazing talent,' I said. 'Being able to visualise something as substantial as a building and then make it real.'

'It is just what I do. You came all the way here from London,' Axel replied, as though hopping on a two-hour flight put creating-entire-buildings-from-scratch into sobering perspective.

'I mean sure, but the pilot did most of the work, to be honest,' I shrugged.

He frowned quizzically, then his face broke into a grin and his shoulders shook with mirth. One massive upside of living in Sweden is that my comedy skills were finally truly appreciated. Bless their cotton socks.

We reached the narrow country road wher lights from little red cottages glowed cosily through the trees. I stumbled on some frozen mud, and Axel easily caught me, his strong hand pinning me to his side as he steadied me. At sudden close quarters, I got a whiff of his scent, something a bit musky and peaty, as though he had been chopping raw wood naked.

Woah. Something I hadn't felt in quite some time sizzled through me, and I drew back with such force that I nearly fell again. 'Sorry,' I muttered, feeling my cheeks burn so much they surely must be glowing in the dark. 'I can take it from here. Thank you. I'm just up this lane.'

'It is no problem to help you the entire way —'

'Thank you, but I'm really fine,' I said firmly. I hobbled away from him as fast as I could.

4

The cottage was in darkness, but the blast of heat that hit me as soon as I opened the door was welcome. I closed the door and pulled the rickety little chain across, hating, yet again, that it was the only available lock. Apparently, there had been a front door key once upon a time, but it had been lost in the midsts of time decades back, and no one seemed troubled to replace it.

I'd been told numerous times that there was no crime out here, but once a Londoner, always a Londoner. I would never be entirely comfortable going to sleep when any Tom, Dick or Harry could wander in with nought more than a vigorous shoogle. For the first few weeks, I had jimmied a kitchen chair under the handle before going to bed, until one night, I forgot. I hadn't bothered since, but only because I forced myself not to think too closely about it.

Feeling a bit unnerved, I limped about, switching on every single lamp and light until the tiny cottage could probably be seen glowing from space. There was an L shaped living area, the kitchen tucked around the corner of the lounge, and the decor was a curious mix of chintzy twee and stark Ikea basics. An open doorway painted baby blue led to a small bedroom and the tiniest bathroom imaginable. It had a mad shower that consisted of a hot water tank overhead that basically dumped on your head when you pulled a lever. After weeks of yowling in frustration as the tank emptied, leaving me soapy for hours until it filled again, I'd finally learned to apply shower gel and shampoo dry, then use the shower more as a rinsing exercise.

I got a fire crackling in the wood burner and sank gratefully onto the lumpy couch, pressed a bag of frozen chopped onions against my swollen ankle. The cool was soothing and I tentatively wiggled my toes, feeling a bit of tension seeping away as one of my favourite fantasies sprang to life in my brain.

We were in London. Me and Johan, and a handful of friends, sprawled on the grass in Vicky Park. Maybe Sarah and Vicks from my junior reporter days on a sadly-deceased free paper in Camden. Perhaps Adam, a DJ I'd become pally with after he saved me from being barred for life from Fabric after getting mouthy with a bouncer of less-than-ideal-feminist standards. Or Kelly, who was one of those mates who just appeared fully-fledged in my life. I had no idea where we'd first met, but she was one of my most important people.

The supporting cast of the fantasy changed up sometimes, but it was always me and Johan, lying on that patchwork picnic blanket I used to have. It would be late afternoon on a stunning summer's day, that magical hour where London is bathed in a pinky-orange glow, and it feels as though everything is right with the world. I'd be leaning against him, sipping from an ice-cold mojito, the kind you get in a can from a fancy supermarket, and he would be toying with my hair. Later we'd stroll home to our flat in somewhere like Shoreditch (no, I have no idea how we afford that, but it's my fantasy, so whatever). It's one of those converted Victorian mansions, and we're in the attic. It's all crooked and quirky and even though there's probably a patch of damp and a drummer living downstairs, we don't care because it's cosy and home.

Would our life have been like that if we'd moved to London instead of Stockholm to be together? The thought weighs heavy on me. I don't even remember the idea of him moving to me ever being in serious consideration, though who knows why. I think I was just so keen to get on with our *happy ever after* that I hopped on the first plane I could.

And look what happened, I thought with a sigh. Sadness drifted over me and I shivered despite the cheery fire. Then I looked up with a soft smile as Johan appeared in the doorway.

'Hey,' I jumped up, wincing as my ankle complained. 'Have you been sleeping?'

He yawned and nodded, leaning against the peeling wood for support. I noticed it didn't creak under his weight. His muscles had faded so much it was almost as though his bones were wearing a Johan suit. His cheeks were gaunt and his eyes seemed sunken into his skull. He grinned, his eyes filling with affection, and the flash of the old Johan sent a toxic mix of sadness and worry and unease darting through me.

'Hey, what happened?' He frowned as I lumbered towards him.

'What? Oh, my ankle. Nothing really, I just tripped over.'

'Sit,' he commanded softly. Johan had been a nurse in another life. A lump formed in my throat as he perched on the coffee table and pulled my ankle onto his lap. With gentle but firm fingers, he prodded his way around the joint, rotating my foot this way and that.

'Where did you fall?'

'In the woods. I was going to have a look at that mad old church. I told you about it, remember?'

'You walked all the way back from the forest?' He glanced up in concern and a ridiculous flush of guilt seeped through me.

No, one of our neighbours helped me, my mind commanded me to say. *I met him at the St Lucia parade and we've been running a handful of times.* It was so ridiculous I'd never mentioned Axel to Johan. It didn't matter. He'd just not really come up in conversation.

Johan planned to come to the St Lucia parade with me that night. It was one of his favourite events of the year. As we'd been getting ready to leave, he told me how he was little they still used real candles for the children's crowns.

'One of my candles was leaning to the side a little bit and dripping hot wax on my ear, but I was afraid I would get in trouble if I disturbed the procession,' he chuckled. 'It was the Katrina church, in Vitabergsparken, you know?'

I nodded. The park was near Johan's flat in Stockholm.

'Anyway, I stood there for the entire event, completely convinced that my ear would be encased in wax for my entire life.'

For some reason, that struck us both on the funny bone. We'd ended up laughing so hard that Johan was then too exhausted to make the walk into the village. He insisted I went anyway. I did, reluctantly, but every time I looked at the kids with their battery-operated crowns, all I could see was him sprawled on the sofa like a deflated balloon, shooing me out the door and making me promise to have some glögg for him.

He placed my ankle carefully on a cushion on the coffee table and wrapped the now-melting onions around it. I leaned forward and stroked his cheek. He smiled, shuffled clumsily to his knees in front of the sofa and wrapped his arms around my waist for a patented Johan bear hug. I melted into his shoulder, forcing myself not to notice how bony it was as his laboured breathing tore at my heart.

'Shall I make some dinner?' I murmured into his neck. 'Although the only problem is, I was going to do Bolognese and I've just ruined the onions.'

Johan sniggered, his breath warm on my neck. We agreed on frozen pizza and he didn't ask again about how I'd made it home on my buggered ankle. Not that it would matter if he had. Johan had never been the type to give a monkey's about a random encounter with a friendly neighbour. I'd got myself a good one, I thought as I limped over to the freezer to rummage for pizza.

I thought I'd lost him.

He had already been slipping from consciousness when I yanked Mia's syringe from his leg. The chaos of police arriving and Mia's followers stampeding faded and distorted like a nightmare as I screamed for help. His face was so white. *We were riding bikes a moment ago.* On dazed autopilot, I launched into the CPR I'd learned from school swimming lessons in the dim and distant past, until somebody pulled me back and paramedics took over.

In the hospital, I was shoved aside as medics swarmed on him in a flurry of barked orders and machines urgently beeping. Somebody brought me into a waiting area, and I think somebody else must have handed me a paper cup of coffee because I was suddenly holding one. I sat for interminable hours on a hard plastic chair, horror seeping into my bones. The idea that Johan was gone danced in front of me, whispering its presence, promising it was just biding its time, as I sat there holding the cold coffee, trying not to scream.

Finally, sometime around dawn, a young man in scrubs appeared. He had been speaking for I don't know how long before I found the wherewithal to wave vaguely and mutter that I didn't speak Swedish. He apologised and explained in halting, precise English that Johan had had a massive heart attack but was now stable.

'Stable?'

My voice was caught in my throat, but my face somehow mouthed the word.

'Yes. He is very weak and his recovery will be long, but he will live.'

He will live. I didn't make a sound. I nodded and sort of crumpled silently into the exhausted young doctor's arms, which he probably could have done without. A few moments later he led me to Johan's bedside.

Johan looked so still, so delicate, dwarfed by machines and wires. The room was dimly lit, which I'm sure was for some important medical reason, but all I could think of was how funereal it was. I was filled with a wild urge to grab the bed and wheel him somewhere, anywhere, more cheerful.

Johan slept for several days. I didn't move from his side, until one morning I shifted just enough to get a whiff of my own BO. I decided that I owed the hardworking nursing staff a shower. It wasn't until I came back, an hour or two later, showered and changed and feeling almost human, that I remembered.

Krister and Mia were dead.

5

The following day, the temperature dropped sharply and the air was filled with snow flurries. I sat by the window at the writing desk, trying to work on the romance novel that was the latest ghostwriting gig my friend and editor Kate had managed to wrangle for me. She was keen for me to pitch another true crime book after the one I'd somehow finished writing about the whole nightmare had done modestly well, but delicious cosy romance was more my speed for the time being. I stared out the window, my mind completely blank, vaguely trying to pretend to myself that I was industriously brainstorming essential story points.

A few months into Johan's recovery, my friend Maddie told us about a couple her girlfriend Lena knew. They lived up here in this tiny coastal village a few hours north of Stockholm, but the woman had just been offered her dream job in the city. I'm not even sure how the conversation went from us expressing mild interest in the fortunes of this random couple to us offering a home swap for six months, but all of a sudden, here we were.

The break from Stockholm and memories of Liv and Krister around every corner definitely gave both of us a much-needed boost, and Johan's doctors had been enthusiastic about the potential for bracing walks in the fresh country air. It felt good. It felt like a fresh start.

But as winter deepened, our energy burst dwindled and stalled. This morning, we'd set out for a walk after breakfast, and between his heart and my ankle, we'd hobbled along like a pair of pensioners. He'd gone for a lie down as soon as we got home, claiming he was just going to the bedroom to read even though I hadn't said a word. When I checked on him a few moments ago, he was sound asleep.

I sighed and stretched my neck. Another chapter and I'd wake Johan for lunch. I was sure it was my imagination he was sleeping more these past few weeks. And even if he was, a neverending Swedish winter took it out of the best of us. This was the most challenging time of the year in Sweden. My social media was full of London friends frolicking in parks surrounded by daffodils and whiling away sunny weekends in pub gardens. I, however, was still debating whether I needed ski gloves or could get away with normal gloves for a quick run to the village shop. Nobody was fine fettle when it was snowing in bloody April. Not Johan, not me, not anyone.

All the same, he must be due a check-up, I thought, making a mental note to ask him when he woke up. The doctors had explained how the heart doesn't exactly repair itself like other muscles. Or rather, it does but so slowly as to make only slight discernible recovery from year to year.

'So I will be clubbing again by the time I am one hundred and fifty years old?' Johan quipped, and we'd both tried unsuccessfully to swallow our sniggers as the cardiologist, a serious woman with thick-rimmed glasses and jet black hair tied sternly back from her face, stonily explained that Johan was unlikely to live that long. With medication and gentle exercise, he should live a full, albeit somewhat slow-paced, life.

'Are you saying that my Olympic dreams are dead?' Johan asked, and this time the cardiologist just stared at him until he meekly apologised.

I had just downgraded my morning goal to *starting* the new chapter, when I spotted a dark coloured car pulling up outside the cottage. Who on earth was that? We were on nodding terms with a handful of villagers, but it was fair to say we didn't exactly have a glittering social life. Other than Maddie and Lena popping up for the odd weekend, I didn't think we'd had a single visitor in months.

A man emerged from the car and frowned at the cottage as though waiting for it to confirm he was in the right place. He wore jeans and heavy hiking boots under a padded rain jacket, and snowflakes settled on his blond moustache as he raised a hand in greeting to me.

I jumped, feeling as though I had been caught. I had every right in the world to be sitting at the window in my own front room staring out.

'Hello, are you Ellie?' The man said in English as I opened the front door.

His gaze came to rest on my bad ankle. Earlier that morning, irritated that the frozen bag — I'd gone for green peppers that day — kept slipping off my foot, I had sell-otaped it to my sock. I'd been quite proud of my inventiveness at the time, but suddenly it looked childish through this stranger's eyes.

'Yes, can I help you?' I said, a bit more shortly than I had intended to.

'I wondered if I might have a word?' His English was

flawless but a little bit formal and stilted. After a couple of years in Sweden, I had begun to tell the difference between people who watched American movies and used English in their day-to-day lives, and those who had studied it at school and rarely used it since.

I wanted to ask what he wanted before letting him in, but the snow was coming down harder. It seemed churlish to make him stand on the doorstep longer than necessary. I stepped aside and closed the door behind him. 'My partner is working in the bedroom,' I said pointedly, just in case this was a very polite home invasion sort of situation.

'Yes, Johan?' the man said, bringing a little notebook out his jacket pocket. My stomach went cold at the sight of the distinct black notebook. Police.

'Have you found Mia? I'll wake Johan,' I said, stepping towards the blue doorway.

'No, no, it's fine, let him rest. I don't know anything about — Mia, did you say? Is she — a family member, or?'

It had felt as though the news dominated every corner of Swedish media, but apparently not quite.

'It doesn't matter,' I said quickly. 'What can I do for you?'

'That ankle looks rather painful.'

'It's fine. I hurt it yesterday, but it's a lot better today.'

'How did you hurt it?'

'I fell.'

'In the forest? Yesterday afternoon?'

'Can I ask what this is about?'

'Of course, my apologies. My name is Karl Lindstedt. I am a police officer. There was an incident at the old church yesterday, and I am speaking to anyone who was nearby, who might have seen something.'

'What sort of incident? What happened?'

'Perhaps you could answer one of my questions before

asking your own,' Karl Lindstedt said mildly, but his smile was firm.

'In that case, no. I didn't see anything in particular, sorry. I just went for a run, and fell over and came home.'

'You saw nobody?'

'No.'

'How did you get home?'

'Oh — sorry, Axel. I don't know his surname. His mum owns the shop in the village, you probably know her. He helped me hobble back here. I assumed you knew that.'

'Why would I know that?'

'I figured he was the one who told you I was there. He's the only one who saw me, so — well, anyway, that's it. I was limping home when I ran into him. He lent me a neighbourly arm.' I heard a strange defensiveness in my voice, though I had no idea why.

'Where did you see him?'

I shrugged. 'I'm not sure exactly, on the path somewhere. Not that far from the road. Maybe a kilometre into the woods, not much more than that.'

'Do you know Axel Pettersson well?'

'No,' I said, too quickly. 'I don't know him at all. Just, like I said, vaguely, from around the village.'

'Around the village,' he repeated as though the phrase were novel and charming. He made a note in his little black pad.

'I've just seen him, from time to time, like you do. He helps his mum at the shop sometimes. He served me glögg at the St Lucia parade.' *Talking like a budgie*, as my mum used to say.

'Then it is quite lucky he was in the forest yesterday, so he could help you.'

'Yes, quite. Very lucky.'

Karl Lindstedt nodded, as though this confirmed something for him, then got to his feet. 'I won't take up any more of your time.' At the door, he paused. 'It is an ingenious idea to tape the ice to your foot like that. Very clever indeed.'

6

I have three favourite runs. One takes me along the coastal path. The beach is rocky and bleak and reminds me of a childhood holiday in Scotland. I remember being wrapped in my mum's oversized knitted jumper, trying to eat ice cream as my nose and cheeks stung with cold. There was a roaring fire in the lobby of our guesthouse, even in July. I loved sitting by it, mesmerised by the flames as my mum enjoyed her pre-dinner glass of wine.

That beach run takes me past the home of the Best Dog in the World. Official. I'm not even a massive dog person. I like them well enough, I'm not a monster or anything. But I'm not one of those people who come running for miles around to greet one, and I hate it when they get up in my face, especially while I'm eating. I once dumped a guy because I swear his dog snogged me more than he did.

But this dog — this dog was exceptional. I had no idea what breed he is, but I'd say part-wolf, part-bear if I had to guess. He is massive. Properly gigantic.

The first time I saw him, lumbering along the side of his house, I was terrified. There are bears in this part of Sweden so it wasn't entirely irrational, though I've been informed that it's been many years since one ventured into the village. *There's a first time for everything*, I thought, frozen to the spot and suddenly yearning for London where the scariest creatures I was likely to encounter were foxes and kids who thought it appropriate to play terrible music out loud on the tube.

Then the dog looked up, and I swear he smiled. He was definitely a dog, for one thing, his thick, dark brown fur giving way to a white, fluffy tummy that just begged to be tickled. He shuffled towards me in a sort of a lopsided manner, as though he were wearing the wrong legs and wasn't quite sure how to use them. He stopped a few feet away from me and just grinned, wagging that massive, floppy tail, until I approached him and patted his head.

A couple of weeks later, I met the owners, a teeny tiny elderly couple who looked like a strong wind would spirit them away. They explained that he had some kind of neurological condition that means his 'brain does not speak very well to his feet,' hence the startling gait.

'I'm not sure my brain speaks very well to my brain a lot of the time,' I'd quipped, and they looked at me with mild, polite judgment.

'Perhaps you don't need to walk in a straight line to be happy,' the old man soberly observed.

That was more philosophy than I'd really counted on during my morning run, but there was no denying that the dog was a huge, floppy, hairy, bundle of pure joy. I took every opportunity to visit him.

The other run loops through the village and around a large, red barn that I am almost certain is used to smuggle some sort of contraband. The barn is exceptionally well maintained, the paintwork flawless and gleaming all year round, but it's just plonked in the middle of nowhere. I suppose that's probably a field behind it, but there is no farm that I can see, and I have never spotted a human anywhere near it. Johan was horrified when I told him I reckoned it was stuffed full of pills. Swedes are adorkably straight when it comes to illicit substances. I'd once mentioned that I did the odd line during my clubbing days, and he asked if I needed to see a counsellor.

The third run goes through the forest and past the old church on the hill. The run I was on the other day when I tripped and yanked my ankle. It was fine now. A couple of days of icing and rest did the trick.

I'll take it easy, I promised myself as I headed out the cottage on the third morning. It was a crisp, frosty day, and I spied a couple of patches of blue sky peeking through the light grey clouds. I broke into a light jog at the end of the path, and turned towards the forest, enjoying the hypnotic rhythm of my trainers against the glistening tarmac. It was a good day. Johan had felt up to a walk yesterday afternoon. We'd strolled through the frosty twilight arm in arm, chatting about nothing in particular, and it had felt like us for the first time in a long time.

As I turned into the forest and felt frozen bracken crunch beneath my feet, I felt a spark of hope spring to life. The sun was high in the sky. It was practically spring. I'm not sure why I had this odd conviction that Johan's heart would be stronger in the summer, but I decided I would just let myself enjoy the optimism. Maybe by the time twenty-three hours of daylight returned, Johan would be recovered and we could finally start our lives together.

Dread prickled down my spine before I consciously registered the sight. I stopped, my ankle already starting to throb as I caught my breath. Crime scene tape fluttered in the breeze, and grim-faced police officers milled around the clearing on the hill. My stomach curdled and my breath felt tight in my chest.

There was an incident at the old church. The church rose above the macabre scene, weathered and crumbling yet somehow defiant against the white sky. My toes had gone numb in my trainers before I realised I must have been standing there a while.

'It looks different on TV, doesn't it?' said a voice, and I jumped.

Axel. He was in running gear, his hands tucked in his pockets as he surveyed the scene as though evaluating it.

'Does it?' I muttered. I knew what he meant. I'd seen enough crime scenes to last me a lifetime.

'Yes, it seems faster, more urgent on those dramas where the police officer always has a drinking problem and a cruel ex-wife. I would expect people to be rushing about, shouting orders. They are more sombre than I thought.' He gave a smile that didn't quite reach his eyes. 'It is respectful.'

'Do you know what happened?'

He shrugged, then frowned at my expression. 'Are you okay? You are very pale. Your ankle, is it still painful?'

'No, it's just — it's nothing. I'm fine. I'd better go. I'm sure the police won't appreciate us nosing about.'

It wasn't until I was almost home that I noticed he hadn't answered my question.

7

'I told you she'd forgotten,' Maddie bellowed when I opened the door of the cottage. The smell hit me about the same time Maddie did. My stomach gave a noisy growl as she enveloped me in a bear hug. A fire crackled in the wood burner and warming spices filled the air. Johan looked up from the large pot he was stirring at the stove, and grinned.

'Of course she bloody forgot,' Maddie yelled. 'We haul our cookies all the way out here to the arse end of beyond, and she forgot.'

'I didn't forget!' I lied through my teeth, and Johan laughed.

'She completely forgot,' he said.

He sniffed at the pot, frowning critically before selecting another spice from the rack and tossing in a generous pinch. Maddie's girlfriend Lena stood at the breakfast bar, pouring four glasses of what looked promisingly like Prosecco.

'Okay, I forgot,' I grinned. I gave Lena a hug and Johan leaned over to peck me on the cheek as I hopped onto one of the stools. 'I should probably shower before joining civilised company.'

'We don't mind you stinking, chook,' Maddie said, knocking back her own Prosecco in one. Maddie was my first — probably my only — friend in Stockholm. When she moved from Australia to be with Lena, she immediately started a social group for newcomers, which met a couple of times a week at a café on Södermalm. I joined when I arrived a year or so later. 'We're here to see you, not be all la di dah.'

'Ellie, take a moment to shower if it would make you more comfortable,' Lena said.

'See, Lena thinks I stink,' I said, and Lena looked stricken.

'Of course I don't think —'

'*Hon retar dig*,' Johan muttered with a laugh.

'Sorry Lena, he's right — I am teasing. But I will take a shower because I can smell myself and it'll put me off my dinner even if none of you mind.'

As I hopped in the shower to rinse off the shower gel, I could hear Maddie launching into one of her mad stories about her even madder personal training clients. She'd been a high-powered lawyer in Sydney, or in her words a 'corporate bitch who wore pencil skirts *on purpose*', but she took the opportunity to reinvent herself in Sweden. She now spent her days cycling between various fancy gyms in posh parts of Stockholm, making an absolute fortune selling people what she called the *Sydney Beach Body*, which, as she reminded us regularly, was not remotely a thing. 'I just yell at them in an Aussie accent and eat it up, bless their bums.'

Johan's booming laugh resounded through the thin

walls, and my heart gave a whoosh like our clanky old boiler starting up. The heat of the kitchen had given his cheeks a healthy glow, I remembered. I'd wanted to comment on him looking well, but, ridiculously, was almost afraid to say it out loud in case I scared it away.

In the bedroom, I grabbed tracky bottoms and a jumper, tying my damp hair back with an ancient scrunchie that almost certainly dated from the period when they were actually trendy. The blind was up, and as I turned to head back to the lounge, a movement caught the corner of my eye. I froze. Then I rolled my eyes at my own ridiculousness. It was my own reflection. Even if there was something in the garden beyond, I'd hardly see it with the light on, would I?

I put my hand on the handle but hesitated, wanting to push the lingering unease away before going back to my friends. It was as though I'd opened a window a crack and the fluttering crime scene tape and solemn officers milling about had slithered in and was swirling around me. I took a deep breath and gave myself a shake. Whatever happened at the church had nothing to do with me. Dinner was ready.

'BUT THE THING WAS, HE DIDN'T SO MUCH AS BLINK. JUST ZERO acknowledgement whatsoever, to the point that I genuinely started to wonder if I might have been imagining him farting with every squat?'

I wiped tears with the back of my hand, my tummy aching with laughter. Lena was chuckling gently. She'd likely heard this one several times before. Johan was in stitches, tears streaming down his face as he literally held his sides. The demolished Moroccan stew sat in the centre of the tiny table. I was mopping up the last of the sauce with a toasted bit of pitta bread.

'Well, at least until the smell hit me —'

'No, Maddie, stop!' Lena protested as I splashed all of our glasses with the remains of the third bottle of Prosecco.

'Christ, I thought I was going to pass out —'

Johan went off into a coughing fit, fighting for breath with a painful-sounding wheeze. I rubbed his back as Maddie clamped her hand over her mouth in horror.

'Shit Johan, I am so sorry. I shouldn't be blethering on like a —'

He held a hand up as he finally caught his breath. 'Maddie, if I am ever too weak for one of your stories,' he managed, his voice hoarse and forced. 'Shoot me in the head.'

'Deal,' she said firmly, but I caught the worried glance she and Lena exchanged and my stomach twisted.

'We went for a walk the other night,' I blurted frantically. 'Quite far.'

'Yes, I will be able to keep up with eighty-year-olds pretty soon.' Johan forced a smile but he couldn't quite keep the bitterness from his voice.

'Johan, I know it must be doing your head in, but your recovery is fucking amazing, you know that, right?' Maddie said. 'I read this article a few months ago in one of the papers. Leading scientists were commenting on the drug she created and how it works so efficiently and instantly to shut the heart down. Mate, the fact you are walking and talking at all is awesome. Don't lose sight of how incredible you are.'

'I did not get the full dose.' He stared at the table. I kept rubbing his back, though the coughing fit was long over. 'What do you call that?' He glanced at me. 'Mates' rates?'

'We should get going,' Lena said quietly. 'The bus leaves soon.'

'No.' Maddie slammed her hand on the table. 'She

doesn't get to ruin this night. She's ruined so fucking much for so many fucking people, I will not give her this fucking night too. I don't care about the bus. I will sit here and tell funny stories until we are all laughing again if it takes until the morning. Got that?'

Johan nodded.

'I'll open another bottle,' I said.

8

I felt it as soon as I reached the village. Something charged in the air. Clusters of tense conversations. A police car parked in the road. A flutter of dread danced in my stomach.

The village was tiny, nestled around the quay where the ferry to Stockholm docked. There was the general shop run by Axel's mum, Pernilla, the kind we'd call corner shop in London. Across the road was a café where you could also buy deli-type food, which I'm told caused great consternation from the owner of the general shop when it first opened.

The library Axel designed sat opposite the shop, next to the café. The building was somehow simultaneously sleek and rustic, neat pine slats forming a kind of bean-shaped structure that always made me think of Dominos lined up, and the roof was a living garden. At this time of year, the garden was mostly a dark green moss, but I could imagine how an explosion of flowers and vines would run gloriously wild in summer.

Once upon a time, I'd thought Stockholm was quiet after

the bustle of London, but the village took *sleepy* to new heights. I don't think I had ever seen more than seven people milling about it at any one time, excepting major events such as the St Lucia parade, when wholesome crowds materialised from miles around. I surprised myself by loving it. I missed the action and zing of London in a sort of abstract way, but after the previous year, the pace of Swedish country life was like a soothing balm.

But today, that was gone. I felt a twist of nerves, which gave me an odd sense of deja vu. I used to get that twist most mornings in London, I remembered. I'd wake up, and tense almost instantly as the day ahead hurtled through my mind.

Three interviews in the morning, all in North London, so I would need to be on the tube by 7:15 to avoid the worst of the crowds while changing branches of the Northern line at Waterloo. I didn't have a break until two, so I'd better grab some crisps or something — maybe at Waterloo if the queues weren't too bad — so I didn't get hangry at my lunchtime interviewee. Forty-five minutes wasn't enough time to file my copy for the evening edition, but it was all I had so somehow it would have to work, and I needed to remember to stuff heels in my bag and somehow get a birthday present before the afternoon's meeting because I'd have to head straight for drinks in Soho. I'd need some kind of sustenance before then or else I'd be smashed on one cocktail, but realistically it would be closer to three before I got lunch so maybe it would do a double whammy, then I'd get a McDonalds for the last tube home and the other people in the carriage would just have to lump it. Oh, and I needed to get to the gym, do some laundry and either learn how to fix a leaky tap or phone someone to fix it. At some point.

These days, the very thought of getting on a tube, never mind at rush hour, made me want to lie down in a darkened room. That old version of me seemed several lifetimes ago. I wondered if I'd lost my edge. I decided that I didn't care.

There was a group of women hanging around the entrance to the café. I vaguely recognised them; I was fairly sure they were a book club or a mums' group that met at the café on a semi-regular basis. I decided that was where I was heading. I tried to make eye contact as I slipped past them to the door, in hopes that I could finagle my way into the conversation.

Not one of them looked in my direction and my brain didn't work fast enough to catch any of their muttered Swedish before I was inside. That little fraction-of-a-second delay before my brain processed Swedish was one of the more maddening aspects of the language barrier. I was a nosy bugger at the best of times, and hadn't realised quite how much I enjoyed eavesdropping on random strangers until the pleasure was removed from my life. The last time I made it home to see my mum, I'd seriously considered doing a lap of the Circle Line just to listen.

The quiet, Middle Eastern guy behind the counter, gave me a nod as I ordered a latte. He seemed friendly but I'd never quite engaged him in more than basic pleasantries. He had an assistant, a twenty-something guy with kind eyes who seemed even more reticent. I wondered if they blethered away nineteen-to-the-dozen as soon as the doors were closed to the general public, or if they worked late into the night baking for the following day, in complete silence.

There was no one else in the café, so I decided to take one of the little tables outside. Fleece blankets were neatly piled up on a basket by the door, and I wrapped one around my knees as I sipped my rapidly-cooling coffee. One of the women at the door glanced briefly in my direction. Knowing it was hopeless, I called '*hej.* She nodded and turned back to her companions.

'*Nej sluta,*' another woman, quite elderly with pure white locks escaping her hand-knitted cap, raised her voice suddenly. '*Skälvklart var det inte mord.*'

My ears perked up. *Of course it wasn't murder.*

'*Det var bara en tragedi,*' she continued.

A younger woman in a thick hiking jacket, long, light brown hair in plaits, shook her head. '*Mord är en tragedi,*' she pointed out.

'*Såna sacker händer inte här,*' the older lady insisted. '*Jag har bott här hela mitt liv.*'

The plaited woman shrugged sadly. '*Men det hände.*'

She was right, I thought, as a chill snaked down my spine. A thing like that had happened here. Somebody died at that church, and whatever the older lady wanted to think, the sheer amount of police swarming around the church yesterday told me it wasn't just an accidental tragedy. I'd done a little poking around online that morning, and Karl Lindstedt was the only full-time officer based in the village. A forensic team must have been called in from Norrtälje or even Stockholm. That wasn't good news.

Things like that may not happen around here, but they did happen around me. A sinking chill of deja vu settled in my bones. So much for finally starting our lives together.

A few minutes later, I spotted Officer Karl Lindstedt striding purposefully past. I knocked back the last of my ice-cold latte and tossed the cup in the bin. Then I started to follow him.

9

The enormous house sat in a clearing deep in the forest. The path I'd followed Karl along wound steeply upwards, and now I could see only sky through the trees. The village sat nestled between two hills on a peninsula that poked out from the mainland like a crooked finger.

As you approach on the Stockholm ferry, it very much looks as though you disembark in the cleavage of a pair of tree-covered boobs. Both Johan and I had been very taken with this when we first arrived, and had spent more time than was strictly dignified trying to get photos of each other from an angle that suggested we were honking our temporary home. Our cottage was at the foot of the inner and more populated, boob, at the top of which was the old church. This house was on the easterly boob that poked out to sea. It was a little higher, I realised now that I was standing on it looking down.

Although dusk was gathering, I could still spot the dark splodge of the church through the bare trees below. I shivered. Whatever the occupants of the house had to do with whatever had happened down there, the fact they couldn't step outside their front door without seeing it chilled me.

The cold had long seeped through my jacket and I hadn't felt my toes in quite some time, but the pathway had forked off so many times I was far from sure I could find this house a second time. I'd manage back to the village, I reassured myself with a bit more confidence than I actually felt. There was only one road to speak of on the peninsula, so as long as I headed in a downwards direction, I was fairly confident I would hit it eventually.

I heard a door slam and jumped. A child, of maybe ten or twelve, kicked the back door behind him then turned and ran across the frosty lawn, heading straight for me. Dirty blond hair hung listlessly to his shoulders, and he wore a thick knitted jumper over skinny jeans. I shrank back behind the nearest tree, but it was too late.

'What are you doing here?' he demanded in Swedish. 'What do you want?'

I cringed and glanced at the house, but there was no sign of an adult following him out.

'*Förlåt*,' I said, wracking my brains for the word for 'lost'. '*Jag, uhm, tog bara ett promenad— en,* I mean, *en promenad —*'

'Nobody walks up here,' he spat in perfect English. 'Why are you lying?'

Despite his sharp words his eyes glistened with tears, so I resisted the urge to tick him off for speaking to an adult like that.

'Why is the policeman visiting your parents?' I asked.

'Why do you care?' His voice cracked and he turned away from me as a sob wracked through him.

'I am so sorry,' I said quietly. 'Here.' I shrugged my jacket off and held it out. I'd freeze to bits, but I couldn't bear to see him sob and shiver at the same time. I was obviously going soft in my old age. He took it with a nod. 'It's a terrible thing that happened.'

'It's not true,' he snapped.

I rubbed my arms as the cold seemed to slither through my skin to my bones. The kid hadn't put my coat on yet. He was just hugging it to himself as he stared at the ground. I was half tempted to ask for it back.

'They are lying.'

'Adults lie quite a lot,' I said, and was rewarded with a hesitant ghost of a grin. 'Especially when the truth is difficult. What are they lying about?'

'Leyla is my friend.'

My stomach gave a lurch. Please no. Not a *child* found in the church.

'I don't need a babysitter,' he added. A sliver of relief ran through me. 'I'm too old.'

'No, you do seem to be very grown up,' I said. 'I'm sure Leyla was happy to be your friend — did she live with you?'

'She lived over there.' He nodded in the direction of the separate garage tucked behind the house. The second storey looked like a perfect little flat for an au pair. I glanced at the imposing building. It was quite newly built, I thought. The entire first floor overlooking a sheer drop to the sea was gleaming glass. The view must be spectacular.

'How long did she live with you?'

'It was only supposed to be for summer when school was off, but then she stayed longer. She was saving up money to take home to Azerbaijan, and Mamma needed a little bit of extra help —'

I was fairly sure that Azerbaijan wasn't part of the EU. I remembered the absolute faff it had taken me to confirm my Swedish residency status after Brexit, and that was after living here nearly two years and with a Swedish partner. I wondered if Leyla had perhaps been on an *extended vacation* in Sweden, paid under the table in board and a pocket money.

'Is the policeman talking to your parents now?'

'Just Mamma,' he shrugged. 'Pappa is working still. Leyla didn't do anything wrong. They shouldn't have sent her away.'

'They sent her away? She was fired, do you mean?'

The kid took a shaky breath, his bottom lip still trembling. 'I don't know.'

'When did this happen?'

His eyes were wide and confused, as though his brain was spinning out of control and couldn't quite process what was happening. He looked so desperately young that even though he was nearly as tall as me, a part of me wanted to pick him up and give him a cuddle.

'Saturday,' he said finally.

It was Thursday now, I thought. Karl Lindstedt visited me yesterday, and Leyla had been found at the church the day before that, Tuesday. Where was she on Sunday and Monday?

'We were going to make pizzas in the wood oven outside and watch a movie, but I waited in the kitchen and she didn't come. I went to look for her, and she was in her apartment packing her things and crying. It wasn't fair' he burst out. 'She always looked after me. I didn't mind that she went out sometimes.'

'Where did she go?'

'It doesn't matter,' he mumbled, kicking at a pile of leaves.

'It might matter,' I said. 'If somebody hurt her, the more we can learn about her life, the better.

He looked up at me sharply. 'You think somebody hurt Leyla? Mamma said she had an accident.'

'I don't know,' I said honestly. 'But it's important we find out. Anything you can tell me about what she did over the past few weeks would be very helpful.'

He kicked the leaves for a moment or two, mulch crumbling over his winter boots. 'She was in love,' he said finally.

'Did she tell you that?'

'Not exactly. She knew she might get in trouble, so she kept it a secret. But I could tell. She was my friend.'

'Sounds like you were a really good friend to her,' I said. 'I'm sure she appreciated you.'

His eyes filled up again and he stared at me, ignoring the fat tear rolling down his cheek. 'She told me one time,' he blurted. 'She said she never thought this would happen to her. She thought she would always be alone, but now she was happy.'

'Did she say anything about the person she was in a relationship with?'

'Just that he was handsome, like a fairy tale prince. All the princes in cartoon movies have huge heads so I asked if he had a big head and she laughed.'

Out of the corner of my eye I spotted the front door opening, spilling light into the gloomy afternoon. I stepped behind a thick tree and kept my voice as low as I could.

'She never said a name?'

He shook his head. 'We only called him Prince Charming,' he said. 'If he is the one who hurt Leyla, I will find him and kill him.'

10

He told her that this had never happened to him. He told her he was typically awkward around women, afraid to even speak to them in case they rejected him. He's really afraid of rejection, he explained. He looked so sad that she wanted to reach out and give him a hug, or at least pat his hand. But it was too soon. It was only their first date.

Then he told her that she was different. He said he had known from the moment they started messaging that he could trust her. 'It's your kindness,' he said, that shy smile tugging at her heartstrings. 'I could just tell that you would never hurt me.'

She felt as though her heart would burst when he said that. Because she was kind. She would never hurt anyone.

Not even to fight back. All those years at school, kids laughing and taunting her, screeching hysterically at the outfit she had thought was lovely when she put it on that morning, or pretending to be her friend just to see if she would believe it. And she did. Again and again, she trusted she had finally made a friend, because she couldn't see why not. She knew she was nice, she knew she could be good fun, why wouldn't this kid or that want to get to know her?

Even when it turned out to be a joke, again and again, she just shrugged and looked forward to the next possible friendship. She joined clubs outside of school, sewing groups and sports teams. She wasn't any good at any of the activities she tried, but she never gave up hope that she would find a friend at the next one or the one after that.

She knew a lot of people. At school, she would tell stories of things that happened on the weekend's trail run or 24-hour read-a-thon, omitting to mention that she had watched quietly at the edge of the drama. Years later, she overheard some kids talking about a school leavers' party she hadn't been invited to. By this point, she hadn't really expected to be asked so she had just been listening with mild interest, but the hostess of the party realised she had heard and turned bright red.

I'm so sorry! It's just that you always seem so busy with your outside friends. I figured you wouldn't want to hang out with us.

That made her realise she might have made a bit of a mistake.

But now, finally, here was someone who got her. Who saw that she was a kind and good person, who wanted to spend time with her because of it.

I bet you have so many men running after you all the time. He shook his head, a blush creeping up his neck that made her want to melt. I couldn't believe it when you agreed to meet me.

She rushed to reassure him, hated the thought that he felt insecure around her of all people, even for a moment. Are you kidding? I was so flattered you even matched with me that I could hardly sleep! It's me who should be grateful. I've never seen a man so handsome in real life, ever.

He chuckled and they agreed that they were both lucky. Then he inched his fingers across the log where they sat until they brushed hers, just gently. Fireworks exploded in her, and she thought she might burst with joy.

Another joke, she thought now. Her throat was raw and sore from screaming and even in the pitch darkness, black spots danced in front of her eyes. She should have known. This was all her fault.

11

I'd been walking on the road long enough that I'd started to worry there was, in fact a hitherto unsuspected second road, when the lights of the village came into sight. The library and café were shut, but Axel's mum's shop was still lit up. Which was a relief, given that it now occurred to me I'd come into the village to get some food for dinner. A quick glance at my phone told me my plans had gone somewhat array.

I hesitated by the water's edge a few moments, listening to the rhythmic splash of the waves smacking the wooden pillars of the dock. I wasn't quite ready for the bright lights of the shop yet. The person found in the church was a young woman named Leyla, I thought as I walked, deep in thought. She came from Azerbaijan and worked as an au pair. She may have had a partner, and the relationship had cost her her job. It was a habit I'd picked up over the years. I'd list the dry facts of a case over and over in my mind. Somehow it helped to distil it down to the essence, as it were. Cut it down to nothing but a list of facts. Nothing scary or overwhelming about a list of facts.

Not that this was a case I was working on, obviously. I was nosing about out of mild curiosity. Force of habit, nothing more.

Skälvklart var det inte mord. Det var bara en tragedi. The woman's words from earlier kept playing in my mind. *Of course it wasn't murder, it was just a tragedy.*

She wouldn't say that if Leyla had been stabbed or strangled. It would clearly be foul play in that case. Had she fallen? I'd got as far as peeking into gaps in the church's walls a few times, and there was a half-collapsed staircase leading up to a small balcony where a choir might once have sat. Was it possible that Leyla had gone exploring and lost her footing?

Or was it possible she had died of sudden, unexplained heart failure?

For over a decade, until I came along, Mia had seemingly lived a normal life, while people around her died of sudden heart failure. Her victims lived with manageable, if life-limiting, conditions, so their deaths were generally put down to natural tragedies. At least, until I started snooping around. This made Mia feel cornered, so she murdered Liv, Johan's first love and best friend. Her fiancé Krister, Johan's other best friend, had died following her into icy water when the police, that I had called, arrived.

I knew that Johan didn't blame me for Liv's and Krister's deaths.

But deep down, we both knew that they would both be alive if I'd just stayed in London.

It wasn't even as though I could say that I'd saved future victims by uncovering her. She had killed several more people before going into the water that night. I had achieved absolutely nothing except lose Liv and Krister and also a significant percentage of Johan's heart and lung capacity.

Just call me girlfriend of the year.

An icy wind snaked under my collar and I shivered. The sea in front of me glistened inky black, reflecting the lights from Pernilla's shop. It was freezing and I should go inside.

It could be her. Accidental tragedy or murder? That was Mia's MO to a T.

Female remains had been found in the water near Krister's a few weeks later, but they were unidentifiable by then. Dental records had been inconclusive. Mia's only living relative, her aunt, had refused to give a DNA sample for comparison purposes, so while an investigation had eventually concluded that the remains were Mia's and declared her dead, there was that tiny sliver of doubt.

I'd asked Lena about it, one evening last summer when she and Maddie came up for a barbecue. We'd belatedly realised we didn't actually possess a barbecue, so Maddie and Johan were determinedly trying to get a fire started in an old tin bucket we'd found. Lena and I sat on the grass watching them, and debating just how soon we could politely order pizza.

'I don't understand why there wasn't any record of her DNA in the system to compare it to?' I asked.

Lena shrugged. 'That is the problem with DNA evidence.' Lena was a police officer. She specialised now in domestic cases and intimate partner violence, but had previously worked in the serious crimes division for many years. 'It only works if the perpetrator is a known criminal.'

'Isn't database of the DNA of every Swedish citizen under the age of forty-something?' I asked. 'I'm sure I've read something about that.'

'The database is strictly for medical research purposes only,' Lena said. 'I believe the police have successfully petitioned for access to it not more than three times in its forty-plus year history. Ellie, Mia is dead. The investigation to identify the remains was conclusive.'

I'd nodded, accepting the logic of what she said, but still —

'Nobody could have survived the temperature of the water that night. You saw her jump in yourself.'

'I thought I did,' I muttered.

'You gave a statement saying you did.'

'I know. I'm not taking it back or anything — it's just that it was all so fast. All I could really think about was Johan — sometimes —' I shrugged helplessly. 'Sometimes I wonder.'

'I think you must try to stop wondering,' Lena said gently. 'I know that is perhaps easier said than done, but Mia is gone. You won't be able to move on until you find a way to accept that.'

But what if she wasn't?

My cheeks stung with ice. Frost glistened underfoot. Out of the corner of my eye, I saw Pernilla lock the shop's front door and stride towards a large 4X4 parked behind. So much for picking up dinner.

What if Mia had somehow survived that night, laid low for months and months and months, just waiting until we felt safe? We'd left Stockholm, but we were hardly in hiding. It wouldn't have been difficult for her to track us down if she was determined. Which she would be. From her perspective, I had ruined her cushty life of living in the open and murdering on the side. I could see that quite clearly.

But then why kill Leyla? She had nothing to do with us.

Then my blood ran cold. Mia's MO had been to execute people she deemed weak or incapable of living a full life. I didn't know if that was the case with Leyla, but it was possible. Maybe it wasn't just about revenge, but picking up where she left off.

Johan.

My throat tightened with a painful twist and I felt pins and needles dance at my fingertips. Johan had a life-limiting condition. He now fit the exact profile of her victims.

Had she followed us up here to kill him?

12

At first light the following day, I was waiting outside the library for it to open. I'd barely slept a wink, and I felt heavy and gritty all over. Johan had been snoring softly beside me, but every time I started to drop off I'd pictured Mia standing just outside the bedroom window. Waiting to strike.

Once or twice I was certain I heard something and crept from bed to peek behind the blinds. It was a clear night and the little garden was flooded with moonlight. It was empty, but I stood there anyway, staring out at the silvery frost for several minutes until my nose went numb from the cold.

The next time I got up I'd jammed the chair under the front door handle. The time after that I made some toast. A blackened log rolled off the glittering embers of the fire as I was getting butter out of the fridge, and I jumped so hard I whacked my hand on the fridge door. I was curled on the sofa wrapped in a scratchy old throw when a faint light appeared on the horizon.

Mia was dead. The Swedish criminal justice system had undertaken an exhaustive investigation and concluded that she died that night. The people involved in the investigation were far more qualified than I to decide these things. But they didn't know Mia like I did.

Finally the librarian unlocked the doors. I settled at one of the workstations and got my notepad out. I'd told Johan I would write at the library today for a change of scenery, and I definitely would. But first, I just needed to put my mind at rest. If for nothing else, I needed to sleep that night.

I wasn't entirely comfortable with how easily the Swedish words for *murder* and *body* and *crime* and *victim* came to mind for Googling purposes, but I pushed that thought away as the results started to load. The first image I recognised was of the crumbling church on the hill. I clicked and began to read. My Swedish was passable by this point. I'd look up a handful of words later to make sure I'd got the details right, but I could grasp the gist with just a skim.

Unfortunately.

Lead settled in my stomach as I read. Leyla had been dead just a couple of hours when she was found in the church by a dog walker. That left Sunday and Monday unaccounted for, I noted. In the tiny local paper, a report claimed she had been displayed in some macabre manner on the altar. An article in one of the national dailies insisted that was nothing but an overactive imagination.

Cause of death was unknown. She had been transported to Stockholm for an autopsy and the results were yet to be made public. I tapped my pen against my teeth as I thought. Officer Karl might know more. The cause of death would be officially *unknown* until confirmed by the autopsy, but that didn't mean it hadn't been apparent to the naked eye. They wouldn't officially confirm, say, a stab wound before the autopsy was completed, just in case the medical examiner found a bullet in the heart. In reality, though, nine times out of ten, if it looks like a fatal stab wound, it is a fatal stab wound.

Cause of death is key, I thought, as I scrolled through snapshots of Leyla, apparently grabbed from social media. If there was a stab wound or strangulation marks, then it was less likely to be Mia. Even after the existence of her drug was uncovered, she had continued to use it, and my gut told me she was unlikely to deviate from that now.

That said, I couldn't find any reference to the mysterious boyfriend. Either the parents hadn't mentioned him to Officer Karl, or the information had somehow been kept out of the press. Or the kid had got the wrong end of the stick, I thought, doodling on my pad as I pondered. If the mysterious boyfriend existed and had not made himself known after Leyla's death was announced. That was a point in the *Not Mia* column.

As was the fact that Mia was dead, I reminded myself firmly. I could well be making a mountain out of a molehill because I couldn't move on with my life. Worse, I could be co-opting the tragedy of this young woman's death and making it about me, I thought, suddenly disgusted with myself. I closed the browser and opened my phone.

No text from Johan, which possibly meant he was still asleep. That was hardly unreasonable. It wasn't as though he had anything to get up early for. The village still had a bit of an early bird feel to it. I was the only patron in the library. Through the window, I could just see a small speedboat of fishermen chugging away from the docks.

My phone buzzed with a text and I was so startled nearly dropped it. I was hopped up on nerves and I'd only had one coffee so far. Maybe I should wander to the café for a soothing camomile tea or something before settling down to some actual writing.

Hej Ellie from England! What are you doing in the library?

Axel. I frowned. How did he know I was in the —

'Are you studying for exams?' Axel grabbed the chair from the next work station and wheeled himself over to me with a grin.

'Hi,' I smiled, glancing quickly at the screen to make sure it was indeed blank.

'How is your ankle?'

'My what? Oh yeah — sorry, it's right as rain now.'

'Right as what?'

'Rain,' I shrugged. 'I've no idea what is particularly correct about rain. I've never thought about it before. But yeah, the frozen peas did the trick and it's fine now.'

'Peas?' he said in surprise. 'Because of the protein, or?'

I burst out laughing. 'No because they're frozen.'

'I see. So we shall go running again?'

I felt myself shift a bit under his gaze. I got a whiff of his cologne and an odd goosebumpy prickle ran through me. I shook my head. I was a ridiculous bag of nerves today. 'Yes, definitely,' I said. 'Sorry, I had a rotten sleep last night so I'm a bit zoinked.'

'I am sorry to hear that. Perhaps we should run tomorrow then.'

'Yes, perfect. Tomorrow sounds great. In the afternoon. I should get some writing done first thing.'

'Okay,' he nodded. 'I have missed your company this week, Ellie from England.'

13

'Ellie!'

I'd just stepped out of the café and taken my first sip of tea when I heard someone calling me. It didn't sound like Axel's voice, but who on earth else knew my name?

I turned to find Karl Lindstedt jogging towards me, a bit red-faced. I stepped aside to let someone else inside the café as I waited for the police officer to get his breath back.

'I always thought that training at the gym was only for vain people,' he wheezed, sweating despite the chill in the air. 'But some days I understand I am wrong in that belief.'

'What can I do for you, Officer Karl?' I asked.

An elderly couple was sitting at one of the café's outdoor tables, watching us with keen interest. 'Would you like to take a small walk?' He nodded towards the docks.

'Not particularly, but alright.'

We strolled up the wooden walkway that jutted out over the grey sea. A tiny tin rowing boat was tethered to the end, knocking against the wooden pillars with a steady thud as it bobbed on the water. The waves were small but furious, sending little white-tipped sprays into the air as they smashed into one another.

'Why did you follow me yesterday?'

Well, he wasn't mucking around. Now that he'd caught his breath, Officer Karl seemed to have regained his composure as well. He fixed me with a steely gaze that I forced myself to return evenly.

'What makes you think I followed you?'

'I think you know I don't have time to play games.'

'Because you're investigating a murder.'

'Why did you follow me yesterday?'

'I wanted to know where you were going,' I replied. I gave a bit of a *mea culpa* shrug, but his expression remained impassive. 'I was in the forest on Tuesday when that poor woman was found, as you know. It freaked me out a bit and I'm curious. I want to know what's going on.'

'So you chose to ask a child instead of me?'

I hesitated. When he put it like that, he maybe had a point. 'That wasn't exactly intentional. I was about to leave when the kid came running out. He started talking to me. I didn't want to run off and abandon a crying kid.' That was true, *ish*.

'You told him that Leyla may have been murdered.'

'Look, I'm sorry. I didn't exactly say it like that, I told him I didn't know —' I cut myself off. A particularly icy gust made my eyes water. I sighed. 'Please, just tell me one thing, and then I will explain.'

He raised an eyebrow that didn't agree, but didn't disagree.

'Did Leyla die of sudden heart failure?'

Surprise danced in his eyes and a chill slithered down my spine. That looked like a yes.

I opened up my phone, pulled up a saved link and

handed it to him. He read it silently, then looked at me blankly. 'Yes?'

'Mia murdered people by injecting them with an undetectable drug that caused them to have an instant heart attack,' I said.

'Yes, I can read.'

'Leyla was in her early twenties if I'm not mistaken. It's fairly unusual for someone so young to have a heart attack out of nowhere, isn't it? Do you know anything about her medical history yet?'

He chuckled and tapped my phone with a patronising smile. 'Ahh, I see what you are trying to say.'

'I think it would be worth your while listening to what I have to say before laughing.' I tried to keep the edge out my voice with little success.

'You think this, woman, this crazy person —'

'I'm not sure that's a term we use anymore.'

'I don't think I am so worried about offending this woman who has murdered so many people,' he smiled. 'You are trying to say that this serial killer has come to stay in our little village.'

'There must be dozens of summer cottages that are vacant right now.'

'Because they are not habitable in winter.'

'But for someone in hiding, any roof over her head —'

'You want me to search our community for a famous serial killer.'

'You have a young woman who died of a mysterious heart attack —'

'That has not been confirmed by the autopsy yet.'

'Mia murdered people by causing instant heart attacks.'

'Diseases of the circulatory system are the primary cause of death in Sweden,' Karl said, with a frown as though he couldn't quite believe he was having this conversation. 'I believe cancer is the second.'

'Not amongst otherwise healthy twenty-somethings.'

'That may not be the case. We have not yet been able to access Leyla's medical records from Azerbaijan. She had not yet attended a *vårdcentral* here in Sweden.'

'I know her.'

'I beg your pardon?'

'Mia.' I reached over and swiped my phone to another article, this one a review of the book I had written about Mia. I hated the photo that accompanied it. It's of me standing on that corner of Katrinavägen where Mia murdered Annette Björkstedt. It was a grey day. Stockholm harbour and city centre sort of melt into the gloom behind me. The photographer caught me frowning as the wind whipped up my hair. I look like a bad actor on a Scandi noir drama, but the publishers in London love it.

'It was me who uncovered her. She nearly killed my partner, Johan, who was her childhood best friend. She had to go on the run because of me.'

His brows furrowed as he skimmed the article, then tapped my phone screen. 'It says here that Mia is dead.'

'Officially, yes, but —'

'I think this conversation is over, Ellie.' He sounded kind, and I bristled. 'Please do not speak to minors about murder in the future.'

'I was honestly just —'

'Thank you for your time.'

With a brief nod, he left me standing alone on the jetty. Well, I fucked that up.

14

When they were teenagers and Cissi was dead to the world until noon at the earliest, Tuva rose early. In summer, the sun was already high in the sky by the time she got up, and in winter it was still hours away. Whatever the season, Tuva never missed six am.

She ate breakfast after her shower, but she allowed herself the one indulgence of enjoying her first cup of coffee in her pyjamas. In summertime she sat on the deck, curled in one of the wooden sun loungers, enjoying the gentle warmth of the sun slowly penetrating the lingering chill of night. In winter, she wrapped herself in a throw and watched the logs in the wood burner crackle and pop as they caught alight.

And that was when she thought of Cissi. Cissi was a coffee fiend, declaring that her greatest dream was to live long enough to see the invention of a designer IV coffee drip, possibly coordinated to match the handbag of the day. While Tuva loved to experiment with different blends and flavours, even becoming partial to the odd creamy latte,

Cissi insisted that anything other than black, strong, plain and freshly ground was an abomination. It was one of the few things they argued about.

So it was entirely correct, then, that Tuva's first coffee of the day was dedicated to thoughts of Cissi. She made it strong and black just as Cissi took it, and once she had drunk the last drip, she closed her eyes and wished Cissi goodbye for another day. Or at least, that was how it had worked for the first few months. As this winter deepened, unrelentingly gloomy and neverending, Cissi started to slip into more and more of Tuva's day.

Despite being physically identical, the twins used to laugh about the fact that they couldn't be more different personality-wise. Tuva was an early bird, while Cissi was a night owl. Tuva industriously studied round the clock to scrape a pass, and Cissi graduated with flying colours after rolling in still half-drunk to most of her exams. Tuva dreamed of settling down with a partner and babies while Cissi regularly changed her mobile number to escape hoards of rejected suitors. Tuva wasn't always the best at remembering things like friends' birthdays, whereas Cissi was famous for her effusive and thoughtful gifts. Yet, all the same, they had never exchanged a single harsh word. Not until that last morning when she had found out what her sister planned to do.

They'd accepted one another for who they were, Tuva thought now as she poked the embers in the wood burner and tossed another log on. People only fought when they expected something more or different from the other and found themselves disappointed. She and Cissi knew who the other was and never expected anything other than what they got.

Tuva sat cross-legged on the mat in front of the fire,

staring into the flames. She held an empty coffee mug in both hands, but had the energy to neither put it down nor make herself a fresh cup. She'd felt *off*, all day today, since the moment she woke up. Unsettled, nervy. She didn't like it at all. Her cousin had been phoning again.

A freelance accountant, Tuva's work was piling up as the tax year drew to a close, but she hadn't quite found it in herself to open up her laptop today. It didn't matter, she thought with a sigh. She would get back on it tomorrow.

Tuva shuddered and put her coffee cup down with a thud. She gripped the mat, forcing herself to take slow, deep breaths to drive the treacherous thought away. She wasn't supposed to think about Cissi coming back. She never allowed herself to hope.

15

I took my time wandering home, turning everything over in my mind to absolutely no bloody avail whatsoever. As I reached the lane where our cottage was, I spotted the dark-coloured car outside our cottage right away, but I couldn't place it for a moment. I started to walk faster. Although my ankle had felt absolutely fine for a day or two now, I noticed I was favouring it as I scurried wonkily across the front garden towards the cottage.

Officer Karl looked up with his usual air of mild disapproval at my existence as I burst in, and I couldn't quite read Johan's expression.

'Long time, no see, Karl,' I blurted as I struggled out my jacket and boots. 'What can we do for you?'

'Karl came by to ask you a little more about Mia,' Johan said, a tight edge to his voice that sent a dagger of nerves into my stomach. 'I explained to him that she has been dead for more than one year.'

'Yes,' I nodded pointlessly as they continued to stare coldly at me. Johan and Karl were sitting at either end of the sofa. I felt that flopping in between them was not the way forward right now, so I perched in the uncomfortable little armchair opposite.

'You seemed to think this was not so earlier.' I couldn't tell if Karl's frown was genuinely puzzled or sarcastic.

'Well, no, I didn't say exactly that, I just said —' I looked to Johan for support, but his expression remained blank. 'They never got the DNA match. I know they concluded it was her, but — I know it's not likely or anything, but do you not think better safe than sorry after everything she's done?'

Johan looked away, but I saw a flash of doubt in his eyes.

'The autopsy has now been completed,' Karl said officiously. 'Leyla died from asphyxiation caused by an overdose of a plant called Aconitum. It is believed she drank a highly concentrated tea.'

I nodded slowly, taking this in. Mia had her own, highly effective drug. An easily detectable poison plant seemed like a downgrade for her. Unless — maybe she wasn't able to make her drug anymore. She certainly couldn't go back to the lab she had created in a disused CIA bunker on Krister's family's property. Presumably, any attempt to purchase any of the ingredients in Sweden would raise some kind of alarm.

'There are, unfortunately, people who believe this plant has healing properties, both physical and —' Karl gestured vaguely. 'Metaphysical. It is not the first time we have had to warn young people from using that church for rituals and suchlike. It was built on a very old pagan site of worship, and for many centuries the village continued to celebrate Midsummer and Valborg there.'

I nodded. That rang a vague bell. 'You're saying Leyla drunk this poisonous tea willingly.' I couldn't keep the scorn from my voice.

'There is no sign anyone else was in the church that

night. No footprints, no trace DNA evidence. It seems that Leyla was alone.'

'Did you find the cup or flask she drank from?'

'Aconitum does not react instantly,' Karl said, but there was a slight hesitation in his voice. 'Even such a strong dose would generally take several hours to result in death.'

'Leyla drank a poisonous tea at home, or wherever she was staying, then hiked up that hill in the dark and rain, then lay down on the altar to die?' I said slowly. 'That is your theory?'

'That is what the evidence supports at this time.'

I flopped back on the lumpy armchair and sighed.

'*Tack för at du kommer,*' Johan was saying as the two men stood.

'*Nej, sätt dig ner,*' Karl gestured for Johan to sit back down. '*Jag kan hitta dörren ensam.*'

Karl shook Johan's hand, nodded to me, then took his leave. For a moment or two, the silence was broken only by the crackling of the logs. Johan was slumped on the sofa, deep in thought. I couldn't read his expression at all.

'What else do you know about this young woman?' he said finally.

I thought a moment. 'She had a partner, or was in some kind of romantic relationship, according to the kid she au paired for.'

'A man?'

I nodded. 'Whoever they are, they must be local, so it would be interesting to know if they have come forward.'

Johan shook his head. 'Karl just told me he has managed to make contact with her family in Azerbaijan. He believes the family she worked for was her only connection in Sweden.'

'The parents didn't mention this relationship to him?' I said.

'Perhaps they didn't know?'

I shook my head. 'The kid said she'd been fired over it. They hadn't liked her sneaking out to meet this person. Unless he misunderstood something. He's only about eleven or so.'

'We need more information,' Johan said. He sat forward, reached for a notepad on the coffee table. 'You could say you are doing research for a book about life in Sweden. You could ask about their lifestyle, their views on personal employees —'

I came to sit next to him, wrapped my arms around his waist and kissed his shoulder through his jumper. 'You're not pissed off with me?'

'About what?' he asked in surprise.

'I wasn't keeping any of this secret from you, I just — didn't know if there was anything worth saying yet.'

'I know.' He kissed the top of my head. 'I know you pretty well, Ellie,' he grinned. He put his arm around me and pulled me close. We sat like that for a moment. 'I do not believe that Mia is alive,' he said softly.

I toyed with the sleeve of his jumper as I tried to formulate a response. It wasn't that I thought she was alive, as much as I was afraid to believe she was dead. That sliver of a chance she could be coming after him —

'I believe in evidence, and only evidence,' Johan continued firmly. I could feel his breath warm on my hair. 'For a long time I worried about the fact that I had never suspected anything strange about Mia. At times I was concerned that Krister was not as happy as I would like my friend to be, and I knew that Liv didn't like her very much, but I never suspected the truth, not for a moment. No gut feeling, no sixth sense. She was just Mia to me.' He went quiet a moment, searching for the right words. He toyed with a lock of my hair, winding it round and round my finger.

'When Krister and I chose our professions, Krister told me that he went into medical innovation because he liked the idea of imagining something and then making it real. You have an imagination like that. You take facts and ideas and you weave them into something new. I am a nurse because I only know how to deal with tangible reality in front of my eyes.'

'Do you think I'm fantasising this?'

'No.' He pulled me closer. 'That's not what I mean at all. I mean you can work in the abstract. You can see a truth that isn't there yet. Krister could do that too.' He took a shaky breath. 'I miss him very much.'

I shuffled up and kissed the side of his neck because I couldn't quite reach his cheek. 'Krister was brilliant.'

'He was. My point is, the evidence I am aware of at the current time tells me that Mia died that night in the water with Krister. But if new evidence arises, I will adjust what I believe accordingly. My point is that I am behind whatever you need to do.'

16

The car roared onto the freeway with a wild lurch and Fritjof closed his eyes. He hated when Pappa drove like this. Pappa always said that he was an extra capable driver and that he had never been in an accident, but Fritjof knew that road safety didn't work like that.

He knew the stats on how likely you were to be in an accident at 100km per hour, 120, 140 and 160, which is what he suspected Pappa was doing now. His stomach twisted up like a huge fist had reached in to squeeze painfully. Prickles of nerves danced through him as the car swerved into the fast lane then back into the middle lane. He was sure he'd felt the tires slip.

Mamma was silent in the front seat, but Fritjof could feel the tension radiating from her in waves. She wouldn't say anything because Pappa would just drive faster if she did. Fritjof turned carefully to look out of the back windscreen, hoping against hope to see the blue flashing lights of a police car.

Pappa would slow down if he got in trouble with the police, Fritjof thought. At least for a little while. And then, as they neared the city, the flow of traffic would dictate the speed anyone could go. He knew that sensible suburban parents in solid Volvos wouldn't concede the lane, no matter how aggressively Pappa roared up behind them. They never did.

But there were no blue lights to be seen. Just white headlights fading one by one into the darkness as they left them far behind. And left their home far behind.

Fritjof clasped his hands together in his lap and held them tightly so they trembled a bit less. He hated the horrible school in Stockholm where no one ever talked to him. He wasn't exactly Mr Cool Dude at the village school either, but at least there were no gangs of bigger boys marauding around the schoolyard. At least it was small enough that the entire school was just one sprawling group of friends that all got invited to everyone's birthday parties and summer cookouts. Everyone split into little cliques at the big Stockholm school, and not one of them wanted Fritjof.

Or at least, that's how it had been two years ago before they moved. He was older now. He'd had two years of being invited to things, of joining in on class jokes and eating lunch alongside kids who were friendly even if he didn't really know what to say to them. Maybe the kids in Stockholm would recognise that. Perhaps this time, the kids would let him join in, or at least not go out of their way to shout about how weird he was.

But even if it was okay this time, he still wished they could have stayed. He liked his teacher at the village school, and he loved his bedroom in what Mamma called 'the glass house'. Most of all, he hated leaving Leyla behind.

Her body was being sent back to her family in Azerbaijan. He'd heard Mamma talking about that on the phone the other day. Fritjof knew it was childish to believe in souls and ghosts and things like that, but he knew that if any part of Leyla remained on earth, it would stay in the village where she had been happy. Leyla's mother was cold, even cruel, and though his mamma could be strange at times, Leyla told him he should be grateful for how nice she was most of the time. She told him she'd never known a real family before she met his. She was happy even before she met Prince Charming.

Fritjof closed his eyes as Pappa slammed the brakes on, and they were all flung forward. A sea of blurry red brake lights spread out in front of them. His chest hurt a bit where the seatbelt had gripped it, but he allowed himself a little smile of relief. The traffic would be heavy all the way into Stockholm now.

Maybe Leyla would visit him in the apartment. She was really clever. She would figure out how to find him if she really wanted to.

17

I cupped my hands against the wall of glass and peered in. The kitchen was one of those sleek space-agey ones, all polished chrome and taps that poured instant boiling water. Many years ago, I trained myself to clean the kitchen in concentrated bursts whilst waiting for the kettle to boil. The idea of the biohazard that would spring up should I ever become fancy enough for such a tap was horrifying.

A loaf of bread sat open on the counter. Toast crumbs were strewn liberally around it, and a wooden butter knife stuck out of a large carton. I'd rung the bell and knocked for several minutes before daring to peek in the windows. The powerful car that had sat in the driveway when I followed Karl here the other day was gone, but they can't have gone far if they hadn't even tidied up after breakfast.

I stepped back a few steps and considered the large, silent house. I wondered if it would be worth waiting. It was mid-morning. A bit late for a school run. The mum could have popped to the village shop, or have met a friend in the café. I liked the idea of getting her alone — it probably wouldn't help my cover story if the kid revealed I'd been hanging around the woods asking about Leyla a few days earlier.

I set my phone timer for twenty minutes and wandered back down to the driveway. It would be just like the thing for Karl to rock up while I was standing on their deck snooping into the kitchen.

I stepped back as far as the edge of the forest and considered the house. It was an odd structure. Stunning, undoubtedly. The juxtaposition of the natural wood slats and clay with unmistakably modern rounded corners and long sloped roof covered with solar panels was striking. It sort of gave the impression of arising from the forest itself, and with a start I realised that it reminded me of the library. I wondered if Axel had designed it.

If he had, he could be a potential in with the family, I mused as I strolled along the edge of the cleared yard. He might have even met Leyla if she had been working for the family long enough, or at least observed her at work. Something about the people who chose to live in this home intrigued me. It was so ostentatious and imposing, yet at the same time tucked out of sight deep in a forest.

Keeping an ear out for the crunch of a car approaching, I slowly dawdled my way to the freestanding garage at the back of the property. There was room for three cars at least. The flat upstairs would be of a decent size, definitely larger than some of the grotty places I'd rented for a king's ransom in London in my day.

A wooden staircase led to a door at the side. Stepping back to the trees again, I calculated that the stairs couldn't be seen from all but one window in the main house. That window was small and round, more than likely a hall toilet.

So Leyla had enjoyed a high degree of privacy from her

employers. I had a few friends who had au paired in their early twenties, and their biggest complaint was having to live under strangers' noses. One, not exactly known for being a homebody, quit after just a couple of weeks when her employers turned out to be stricter than her own parents.

My toes had gone numb in my boots by the time the timer buzzed. There was no sign of anyone coming home. I gave the house a final glance and started my hike back down to the village.

'No luck,' I announced to Johan, hanging my jacket on the hook. He was on the sofa, sitting up straight, poring over his laptop. The coffee table was strewn with a notebook and at least two empty coffee cups. He looked — alive, I thought. Obviously he had been alive the whole time. *Engaged*. That was it. For the past year, it was as though he had been floating at the edge of life. Observing it from a distance, dipping in now and then, but not properly deep in it. Not getting his hands dirty. He was fully engaged, getting his hands dirty now, I thought as I flopped on the sofa next to him.

'They weren't home. I'll try again later, or tomorrow.'

'Look at this,' Johan said. He tilted his laptop so I could read it. 'Another young woman went missing. Not here in the village, but just a few kilometres further up the coast. Cissi Hallström worked as a nanny in Stockholm,' he said. 'She and her sister were orphaned after a car crash when they were teenagers, but her sister still lives out here in the home where they grew up. Cissi stayed a few weeks with her sister after Christmas because she was between jobs. I looked at a map, and their property is just beyond the mouth of our peninsula, so to speak. You could walk all the way through this forest and reach it, though it would take some hours.'

'Is she still missing?'

Johan shook his head. 'It does not appear she has been found, but there is no investigation because the sister never officially reported her missing. She was supposed to be going to a new nanny job in Hong Kong. Initially, it was assumed she had simply left to take it up. It wasn't until months later that a cousin tried to get in touch with Cissi and discovered she had never arrived to start the job,'

'Surely she had been in touch with her sister?'

'They had a falling out the morning Cissi was due to fly. It seems Cissi was well known for not bothering to contact anyone for months at a time. The cousin describes her as *the kindest person you could hope to meet — when it suits her.* Cissi had gone travelling after high school and the family had only known she was alive through social media posts every few weeks.'

'Did she say goodbye to the sister and then disappear somewhere between here and Hong Kong? Do we know if she got on the flight?'

'The sister refused to report her missing to the police. That is why the cousin went to the media in desperation. Without a police warrant, the airline couldn't or wouldn't release passenger names. Apparently, the sister insisted that Cissi probably met a man on the plane and changed her plans without telling anyone.'

'For over a year?'

'This article is from this Christmas, but I found the cousin's Facebook, and she posted the latest appeal for information about Cissi just two weeks ago.'

'So she is still missing. Does it sound from the post as though a report has since been made to the police?'

'No. Part of the post is begging Tuva — that's the sister — to reconsider. But Ellie— look at the date she disappeared.'

I leaned over his shoulder to read and a chill washed over me. Cissi was due to leave for Hong Kong the same day that Mia went into the water.

18

Tuva Hallström's house was a neat, modest family home on a small cul-de-sac at the forest's edge. It backed onto the water, and I could just spy flashes of colour from neighbouring houses through the trees as I approached. The front garden was well-tended, with some early wildflowers starting to poke through the gloom, and neatly prepared topsoil awaited seeds along the boundary fence.

I couldn't see a doorbell, so I knocked. There was a small blue car sitting in the driveway, and I could see the glow of a lamp through the front window. I waited a few moments, then knocked again.

Johan had managed to get the cousin, Linda Hallström, on the phone last night, and I listened as he sympathised about how Tuva was an unusual personality and that Linda had been as patient with her as she could before going to that journalist out of desperation. Tuva needed kindness and understanding, Linda explained, but not at the expense of Cissi's safety.

I knocked one more time, a sharp rap to hopefully

convey that I meant business. After a few moments, I heard footsteps. They paused, maddeningly, for several long seconds before finally hearing the jangle of a key chain being drawn across and the click of a lock.

'*Hej*' I said with a bright smile as Tuva Hallström regarded me warily. '*Är det okej på Engelska?*'

*P*retty much every Swede spoke flawless English, but it seemed like manners to ask before wiring in.

'*Nej,*' she replied.

'Oh —' Well shit, I thought in panic. That I had not accounted for. I was here now, I was just going to have to manage as best I could.

'My name is Ellie,' I said in halting Swedish. 'I would like to talk to you about your sister, Cissi, if that is okay?'

From her expression, I deduced it was most definitely not *okej*.

'Why?'

I desperately scanned my brain for words, half wondering if steam was coming out my ears. 'I want to help.'

'Help? What does that mean?'

'Find her,' I stammered. 'I want to help find her.'

'How do you know where she is?'

'I — not know — but if I may ask questions, I can try?'

'Try?' she repeated, her voice dripping with condescension.

'Please — may we speak together? With — little information, I can try.' Yeah, I should really have paid a lot more attention in Swedish class over the past couple of years.

'What information do you want?'

'Can we go inside and talk — with me?' That wasn't even right in English, I thought in frustration. What was it about Swedish that broke my brain?

'We can talk here.'

Fabulous. To be fair, this conversation wasn't going to be any less excruciating sat on a sofa. Even though the journey from our cottage was barely ten kilometres, it had taken two busses and included quite a long wait for the second one at a desolate, shelterless stop, so it made sense to come alone. It might be worth splashing out on a taxi to bring Johan another time to speak with her like a functional adult, I thought. On reflection, at this rate I was far from confident Tuva Hallström would ever open the door to me again. I had to get what I could, while I could.

'Did your sister take her things to Hong Kong — in a suitcase? Clothes and like? She put them in bags before she left?'

'Of course.'

'And she said goodbye the morning of her flight and left for the airport. You did not go to airport with her?'

'No.'

'You didn't go?'

'No.'

'But she said goodbye?'

Tuva hesitated and glanced away. 'She left for the airport.'

'But you are not sure? You did not see her leave in taxi, or?'

'She left. I saw her leave.'

'Okay, thank you. She had friends here? In town? High school?'

'Cissi had many friends. Some still lived here, yes.'

'Their names? I can take their names?'

'You said you wanted information from me.'

I pasted my smile firmly on. Maybe Johan could do some social media stalking to identify these friends, or perhaps it would be possible to track down former students through the high school's website.

'Of course. Did Cissi have a guy? Romantic, I mean.' What the hell was the word for boyfriend again? 'Partner?'

'Not a partner,' she said, and it seemed that she slightly stressed the word *sambo,* which normally denoted long-term, live-in partner.

'But a guy? Friend? Boyfriend!' It had come back to me. It was literally a direct translation of boy-friend. 'Did she have any boyfriend?'

'Not that she told me.'

But she suspected, I thought.

'Cissi has hundreds of boyfriends and fuck-buddies,' she added bitterly. 'She was supposed to be spending the time with me. Cissi is very selfish.'

'But she spent time with a man? Before she went away?'

Tuva looked away, but I caught an infinitesimal shrug of assent.

'You did not phone the police?'

'The police are not helpful.'

'Your cousin —'

'Linda does not know Cissi like I do,' Tuva spat. 'Linda visited us once, twice a year and sent gifts at Christmas since our parents died. She thought that made us family, but only Cissi and I were family. We were alone since our parents left and nobody cared but us. Cissi left. She found a new life. Cissi does whatever she wants.'

It took me a moment to process that, and by the time I got the gist, Tuva was still staring at me furiously, her chest rising with heavy breaths. She was telling the truth, I realised. Or at least, the truth as she knew it. Rightly or wrongly, Tuva believed that her sister had willingly taken off and not been in contact for over a year.

'I am very sorry,' I said.

I started the long walk back to the bus stop, belatedly realising I'd forgotten to check the return times. Tuva was shattered by her sister's disappearance, I thought, remembering the anger and grief that had flashed in her eyes as she slammed the door in my face. But she definitely wasn't concerned about her. In fact, I realised with a chill, Tuva Hallström absolutely hated her sister.

19

'It makes noz difference,' I insisted.

'Ellie, I am questioning our entire future together.' Johan shook his head, his expression stricken, as I blocked his path to the fresh pasta shelf in the village general store.

'By the time it is cooked in a lovely sauce, it tastes exactly the same.'

Johan met me at the bus stop in the village when I got back from Tuva's, and we'd decided to have an early glass of wine before picking up some dinner. I filled him in on my impression of Tuva. Apparently, Cousin Linda believed she probably should have been diagnosed with a neurodivergent condition as a teenager, but the parents' deaths had thrown the twins' lives into such disarray that concern over Tuva's communication skills had fallen by the wayside. We debated whether or not it would be worthwhile going back together.

'I don't think I missed anything she said,' I said, thinking the frustrating conversation over. 'My understanding is pretty fluent now, even if my own vocabulary is lacking. The questions I asked her were phrased a bit clunkily, but she clearly knew what I was saying. Let's keep it as an option to go back if we come across anything more about Cissi.'

He nodded. 'Do you think she could be worried about her but not comfortable about expressing that to you?'

I shook my head slowly. 'I could be wrong, but my honest impression is that Tuva has washed her hands of her sister. She resented me invading her peace for sure, but I'm convinced her anger is directed at Cissi. I'm guessing they had some massive fight, and Tuva believes Cissi has willingly chosen not to contact her in over a year.'

I toyed with the stem of my wine glass. There was another couple at the table closer to the bar, and the quiet man who ran the place had just lit little tea lights on all the tables. Johan's hand rested on my knee as he sipped his own wine. 'It was kind of dark, if the truth be told,' I added. 'I'm not sure Tuva Hallström is a very nice person.'

'Ellie,' Johan begged now. 'Please, think of what you are saying. Do I mean nothing to you?'

'You do, but fresh pasta does not.' I stuck my tongue out at him. 'I won't stop you buying it, my friend, but you should know that it makes no difference. The whole thing is a con by — Big Spaghetti.'

He shouted with laughter, and the elderly man considering cheese next to us looked around in surprise. 'Big Spaghetti?'

'Big. Spaghetti.' I nodded meaningfully. 'Educate yourself.'

'You're not the boss of me,' he whispered, like a movie mafia don, then tossed two packets of fresh pasta into our basket.

I giggled, and we moved on to argue about vegetables.

'Ellie?'

'Axel, you startled me.' We'd come round the corner and I'd pretty much smashed smack dab into Axel, who was now giving Johan a curious once over.

'Axel, this is Johan, my *sambo*,' I said quickly. My voice sounded a bit high and tight to my own ears, which was ridiculous. 'Johan, Axel lives here in the village. This is his mum's shop.'

'It is a good shop,' Johan smiled. 'Great pasta.'

'Ellie and I go running sometimes, also,' Axel added.

Johan nodded without much reaction, because he is Johan. I wanted to squeeze his hand, but something stopped me from reaching out. There was something about Axel's manner I couldn't quite put my finger on. He usually had an easy, relaxed smile, but he was staring at Johan warily, as though he half-expected him to challenge him to a fight or something.

'*Trevligt*,' Johan said, a peculiarly Swedish quirk wherein they shorten 'nice to meet you,' to 'nice.'

Axel nodded in return and then turned back to me. 'I thought we were going to run this morning?'

'Shit, I completely forgot. I'm so sorry, I got distracted with, uhh work and whatnot. I should have texted you. I am sorry.'

'Another time,' Axel said with a shrug. 'Maybe you should rest that ankle a little longer.'

Johan glanced at me, obviously curious that Axel knew about my ankle, and I could have sworn that Axel's smile was a tiny bit triumphant.

'Axel helped me from the woods when I fell that night,' I said firmly. I took Johan's hand, interlaced my fingers with his. 'I was lucky he was there, don't know how long I'd have been hobbling away like a —'

'A lame wood nymph,' Johan supplied.

'Exactly. It would have been terrible.'

'Then I'm glad he was there too.'

'Oh Axel, I meant to ask you,' I said as he started to turn away. 'I came across a stunning house the other day, in that part of the woods.' I pointed up the hill. 'Did you design it? It looks like your style. It's really amazing. Axel is an architect,' I added to Johan. 'He designed the library.'

'The library is beautiful.'

'Thank you,' Axel said with a brief smile.

'Do you know the family who live there, at the fancy house?'

'No. My clients were the previous owners.'

'We should have you to dinner sometime,' I blurted. 'Next week, maybe?'

'That would be very kind,' Axel said tightly. He gave Johan another cold glance. 'Nice to meet you.'

With a brief nod, Axel left us and I shrugged at Johan. 'That was odd. He's normally really nice.'

'To *you*,' Johan grinned, seeming pleased as punch.

'I beg your pardon?'

'He loooooves you,' he singsonged under his breath like a twelve-year-old.

'Get lost, you giant idiot.' I whacked him with one of the packets of pasta.

20

Memories are what make us human. She had read that, somewhere, once upon a time. Animals have short term and specific memories. They can remember where their food comes from, or recognise a place of danger a long while later. But they don't have abstract memories. They can't recall events in their pasts. Only humans can do that.

She remembered laughing about that. She envied monkeys and elephants not lying awake, berating themselves about something stupid they said or did. How pleasant must it be to live completely unaware of having once annoyed or confused somebody.

Maybe she was turning into an animal. Maybe that's what happened, after long hours and days of solitude in complete darkness. Maybe the complexity of human psychology reverted to something more primitive. Perhaps, as time dragged interminably forwards, she was being dragged backwards into a simpler, baser form.

It was true that she was no longer concerned with how stupid she had been to think he wanted her. That sort of abstract concern had floated away into the ether. Who cared whether *anyone had ever wanted her? She didn't. The importance of other people, the validation she had once craved from them had melted into this timeless state of gnawing terror in which she lived now. Who were other people, anyway. What did any of them matter to her?*

All that mattered was her hunger. She needed to get something into her stomach. A tin of ice cold water at her feet tasted stale and a bit metallic but quenched her thirst. She was almost sure she had drunk it all several times, but that would mean someone was refilling it while she was sleeping, and she didn't want to think about that.

Had there been some bread? There must have been because she wasn't dead, and she had been here forever. She must have learned once how long the human body could survive without food. It felt like the sort of thing a person should know. A few days? A week? She had been in the darkness at least that long.

Hadn't she?

She closed her eyes and tried to think. She needed to feel one memory. Any moment in her entire life up until the darkness. There must be one. She knew she had lived. She was aware, in an abstract way, that she had gone to school and trained as a hairdresser and —

There it was. A clear recollection floated from the abyss. Her first day on her first job. She had been tasked with washing clients' hair before they went to a fully trained stylist for their cut. Unused to the over large bottles, she had accidentally put three times as much shampoo as necessary on a stern-looking lady. She'd watched in horror as the bubbles seemed to froth up, down the lady's face and into her eyes. The lady had jumped up, flailing blindly for a towel as she released a torrent of abuse at her incompetence.

She smiled into the darkness, a flush of joy running through her. She could see the lady's face, hear her furious screams, picture the manager apologising profusely and shooting angry looks. She could feel her own horror as terrified giggles rose up and burst out, and she started to giggle again in the darkness.

She had remembered. She was still human. She was surviving.

She heard a clink of metal ping through the blackness and she froze.

21

'Do you think it would be possible to find out whether Cissi ever got on that plane?' I mused as Johan unpacked groceries and I fiddled about setting the fire. 'I'm quite sure passenger lists are confidential, but the police can access them with a warrant.'

'But without an official investigation I guess they won't.'

'There's a thing you can do in the UK, I can't remember the exact term, but it's like an expression of concern — it's short of reporting someone missing, but you can have the police do a wellbeing check on someone. I think it can be used in suspected domestic abuse cases, for example. If Linda can't have Cissi declared a missing person while Tuva insists she is fine, I wonder if she could do that? For all we know, the Swedish embassy in Hong Kong could find her perfectly well, exactly where she said she would be.'

'I don't know if that exists in Sweden, but if it is used in domestic cases, then Lena would know of it,' said Johan. He salted a pot of water on the stove and set it to boil.

'Even if it doesn't, she might be able to do a bit of nosing anyway.' I hopped onto the breakfast bar and watched Johan slice tomatoes. 'If Linda is right to be worried about Cissi, then we're looking at two missing women in a reasonably small, remote area, both of whom worked with children, both of whom were possibly in new relationships — and neither were reported missing. Nobody knew Leyla was gone until she was found, and Cissi's relatives still can't agree.'

'But only one found at the church.'

'So far,' I said. 'It's not uncommon for killers to up their game, so to speak. They might have intended to kill Cissi at the church but something went wrong and they panicked, or they chickened out of displaying her on the altar for whatever reason, but the second time —' I trailed off, horror filling my guts.

'What?'

'What if it's not the second time? A whole year is a long time, and it's —' I cut myself off, struggling to find the right word. 'It's *polished* this time. It's quite a leap. The killer would have had to walk or carry Leyla through that forest. Even at night there was a chance they could have run into an insomniac dog walker or something. If they persuaded her to drink the tea elsewhere, they must have known how long it would take to work to time getting from wherever they were to the church —' I shook my head. 'It suggests confidence. It suggests they had experience and knew what they were doing.'

'Unless Karl is right and she mistakenly drunk it herself,' Johan said gently.

The police in Stockholm believed Sven Olafsson, Annette Björkstedt, Cattis Bergman, Sigge Åstrand, and Björne Svensson died of natural causes, leaving Mia to work in peace for ever a decade.

I sighed. 'Yeah, maybe. I'll ring Lena in the morning,' I

said. 'Let's see if we can find out if Cissi was on the plane to Hong Kong, and take it from there.'

'In the meantime, I will cook this fresh pasta.' Johan leaned over the counter and pretended to bite my nose. 'And I will prove you wrong about it.'

I chuckled. By silent agreement, we changed the subject as he started to cook and I helpfully contributed my wine-pouring skills. I told him about the time my friend and I busked outside a club in Sydney to raise enough money to buy ourselves proper shoes because they wouldn't let us in wearing flip-flops.

'I've heard you sing, Ellie.' He raised an eyebrow as he stirred the pasta sauce.

'Yes, they paid us to stop. By the time it occurred to us that there weren't any shoe shops open at 10pm, we'd made a couple of hundred dollars. We went to this beachside bar that didn't mind flip-flops and bought a round for everyone there. And then we wrote a musical about a botched breast enhancement called *One Big Boob*.'

Johan snorted with laughter and poured the pasta into the bubbling water. Then he went quiet a moment, and I noticed he was holding onto the counter for support. I wrapped my arms around his waist and hugged him from behind, feeling him tremble as he struggled to catch his breath, wishing desperately that I could somehow pour some of my strength into him.

'Shall I finish dinner?' I asked softly. 'There's nothing left I can destroy, right?'

He took a breath that was still a bit shaky but stronger. 'It's nearly done,' he said.

I knew better than to argue, so I put the TV on and flicked through the movie service, trying to find a screwball eighties comedy. Something with John Candy or Steve

Martin, I decided. Johan poured the sauce over the pasta and I brought the plates over, leaving him to bring the breadbasket.

A few more flicks and I found the kind of movie I was looking for, something about Boy Scouts having whacky mishaps on a camping trip.

'I always wanted to be a Boy Scout,' Johan said. I tucked in to the admittedly delicious pasta, doing my best not to notice that he hadn't taken a bite yet. 'American movies make it look so exciting and adventurous.'

A kid was hanging precariously from a branch by the waistband on the screen, gravity slowly tugging his shorts down.

'You aspired to mooning your friends from a tree?'

'I did.'

Johan's phone lit up with a Facebook Messenger notification. He reached for it and held it up so we could both see. 'Linda.'

'Tuva's cousin?'

'After we talked the other day she sent me a friend request,' he shrugged. He opened the message.

CISSI HAR TEXTED!!! It read in capitals. *HON LEVER! HON ÄR BRA, HON ÄR FRISK OCH GLAD!!!*

She lives, she is doing well, she is healthy and happy.

He scrolled to the second message, in which Linda explained Cissi had indeed been waylaid while changing flights at Heathrow, and was living on a Thai island with her now-fiancé. She would bring him to Sweden to meet Linda and her family as soon as possible.

I looked up at Johan and our eyes met with identical expressions.

'Helluva timing,' I said.

22

The following day, the wind was bitter when I reached the old church. Trees swayed, one or two even creaking ominously, and a few particularly jaunty gusts nearly took my breath away. I slowed down as I reached the clearing and surveyed the ruin. I'd texted Lena to ask if she had a moment to chat today, and she'd replied saying she was in back-to-back meetings all day but would ring if she got a moment. Then I'd headed out a run after breakfast and found myself drawn to the church. It couldn't hurt to look at the spot where Leyla was found.

The wind shrieked with particular force and I shivered. It was such a bleak spot. The church looked almost black against the white sky; the trees all around were skeletal and bare. There was little sign that it had ever been a crime scene, which was worrying. I could almost feel *senseless tragedy* settling over the matter.

Steeling myself, I approached the church slowly. I'd never been one for nightmares, or what my grandma used to call the willies. 'I don't have even ONE willy,' I'd reply indignantly before collapsing in giggles. Grandma would ask

Mum if she'd thought about having me seen to by a professional, and my long-suffering mum would roll her eyes and mutter something about hormones.) I loved a good horror film, sat through funfair ghost rides stony-faced, and I'd been the only one in my fifth year English class to be entirely untraumatised by *The Woman in Black*.

I mean, it was a perfectly good story, I just didn't give it another moment's thought once I put the book down.

But there was nothing like a desolate murder scene ransacked by shrieking wind to make you wonder if you had a willy or two after all. That brought forth a snigger, which made me feel better. Relief that I was as mature as ever brought forth just enough courage to clamber over the pile of rocks that had once been steps leading to the church.

There was no longer a door, though there was a cluster of rust in the stone frame that made me think there might have been hinges once upon a time. I crept forward, hearing my own heartbeat resound in my ears. Water dripped from somewhere out of sight, echoing over the howl of the wind. Although there were enough holes in the structure to make it barely feel indoors, somehow the wind was a bit muffled, which further added to the disconcerting sense I had entered another dimension.

Firmly pushing any notions of walking up the aisle to marry an evil demon lord of the underworld out of mind, I slowly approached the altar. A bit of effort had been made to tidy up, but I could see the area that had been cleared around where Leyla must have been found. A few dustings of what I presumed to be fingerprint powder were scattered nearby.

The recent presence of a twenty-first-century police investigation was oddly reassuring. I slowly walked around what had been the epicentre of the crime scene. The three steps up to the altar area were surprisingly intact, though moss and vines had reclaimed most of where a pulpit must once have stood.

A faint scratching, scurrying sound hit my ears as the wind died down a moment, and, in a plot twist I'd never have predicted, I very much hoped it was indeed rats. Looking up to what remained of the ceiling, I could see that various small holes must create a bit of a dappled effect over much of the church on a sunny day. A wide gap awned over the altar, and as I stepped back, I could see that the sun would flood the cleared space, spotlighting where Leyla had lain.

I sighed with frustration. I don't know what I'd expected. Graffiti, maybe, *Mia waz ere*, helpfully scrawled on a crumbling wall.

The whine of a speedboat cut through the racket of wind. Curious, I went over to the largest gap in the wall, clambered as lightly as I could up to a sort of pile of rocks moonlighting as a windowsill. The hill on the other side of the church sloped steeply down to the choppy sea below.

The village side of the peninsula faced a sheltered bay. Other than a deep-ish channel that allowed the Stockholm ferry to approach, it almost felt as though you could wade to the nearest archipelago islands if you were of a mind. But over here, I was looking out over vast, foreboding sea. It was a sort of dark-blue-grey, white-tipped here and there as it grouched out towards the horizon, and presumably Finland beyond. Just the sight of it made my bones ache with cold, and for an instant I almost felt it rushing over my head, ice-cold and heavy, dragging me down, filling my lungs as I clawed in vain towards the surface. I'd never been what you'd call a fan of water, another reason that moving to city spread over several archipelago islands hadn't been my cleverest idea. Driving Krister's rickety little speedboat to his family's island to find the hidden lab where Mia created her murder drug wouldn't have been my first choice to address that particular phobia, but I had to admit it had somewhat done the trick.

I couldn't see the boat yet, but the whine changed to a sort of chugging noise. I stood on tiptoes, holding onto a damp, freezing stone to lean out, until finally, I caught sight of the boat. It was vintage, made from sleek and gleaming wood polished a warm reddish colour. It cut through the churning waves, bobbing alarmingly from side to side. A man stood at the steering wheel, carefully negotiating the angry water.

Axel, I thought in surprise.

I don't know why I was so taken aback. He'd never mentioned owning a speedboat, but why would he? On our handful of runs, we mostly chatted nonsense about nothing in particular, more often than not, running in companionable silence. I didn't know anything much about his life.

Yet for some strange reason, I felt a bit — thrown. Even a tiny weeny bit hurt. With a jarring crunch of gears, Axel turned the boat so that it was horizontal to me, and icy chills dashed over me. A woman sat in the seat behind him. He'd definitely never mentioned a girlfriend.

Wife?

Friend with benefits?

I stumbled backwards, mortified at the idea they might glance up and catch me perving on them like some kind of a weirdo. I felt all flustered and clumsy, which was basically how I spent the entirety of my teenage years, hanging at the edges of clubs watching boys I fancied snog other girls.

Obviously, this was nothing like that. I was a grown

woman with a partner I loved very much. Axel was a running buddy who barely registered in my life. I just —

I suppose it wasn't as though I had many friends in Sweden. There was Maddie, who was a delicious, loveable, entirely open book, and —

Well, I'd once thought Mia was my friend.

I supposed I was allowed to be a bit sensitive when it came to Swedish friends keeping secrets from me. Not that Axel had kept it a secret, as such. I'd never directly asked him if he was in a relationship.

I clambered over piles of rubble, skidding in my haste to reach what remained of the door.

Axel was a bit of a flirt, I supposed. He didn't exactly have a *taken* vibe. I'd told Johan not to be so ridiculous last night, but the truth was, I'd sort of suspected Axel had a little thing for me. Not that I'd wanted him to, obviously, I just felt a bit stupid for getting it so wrong. My ego was feeling a mild, inconsequential bruising.

Feeling a sudden urgency to far away from this horrible church, I hurried down the hill.

23

It was so hot the sand burned the bottom of her feet, but she didn't care. She ran lightly all the way down the pristine, white-gold beach and waded into the lukewarm, aqua water. The relative coolness of the water was a relief after the unrelenting sun, and she dipped all the way under then stretched out to float on her back.

This was paradise, she thought, then she laughed at herself. What was the word Fritjof would use again? Basic. Of <u>course</u> a beautiful beach on a hot, sunny day was paradise. She wasn't special for liking something so obvious.

So let me be basic, she thought with a laugh out loud that echoed through the still day. She watched that huge, deep blue sky, unbroken by a single cloud, stretch into forever above her. The water bobbed gently and she was rocked from side to side.

She liked the feeling. Even though she knew that people drowned every year, she felt safe, cradled by the water. Nobody drowned in water like this, she decided. This water was only kind.

And even if she drowned, she wouldn't mind. She heard a

little ripple as a fish leapt or a bird dove. She would be happy to exist in this water for all eternity.

Though why was she even thinking about that? Why would anyone think about something like death on such a beautiful, perfect day as this? She exhaled firmly, the way she had been taught in a yoga class, once. Release all the bad thoughts into the universe. There you go, universe, she thought with a smile. Good luck with all my bad thoughts.

She wasn't going to have any more bad thoughts. She was just going to lie here and float. She would feel the warmth of the sun and the water and she would think happy thoughts and be glad and grateful.

An icy wind snaked around Maarji, and she started to tremble violently. The sun and the sea evaporated and there was only cold, forever darkness. No, no, no -- come back, she thought desperately. Don't leave me. I don't want to be here.

She tried to scream but her voice was long gone. Maybe it was on that warm beach. She would go back there, she decided firmly. That was where she would be now.

She closed her eyes and felt the warmth of the sun beating down. She was going to get a burned nose, she thought with a laugh. She didn't care. She ran across the burning sand and splashed her way into the water.

24

'Officer Karl.'

He gave me a wary look as I fell into step with him.

Daffodils had sprung up, seemingly overnight all the way along the road to the village, and in the clearing behind the general shop, a large Valborg bonfire was being built. Whether it was just relief to be away from the church, it did feel promisingly as though spring was in the air. *About bloody time, Sweden*, I thought. Monday would be the first of May.

Valborg was Sweden's pagan answer to Bonfire Night. The spring festival completed the set of Midsummer, Halloween and Yule, though it came with a disappointing lack of fireworks. I knew it was no longer trendy to like fireworks. I didn't actively wish dogs any fear, but I'd always be a sucker for a winter's sky exploding with twinkly lights. The thought reminded me of the Best Dog in the World, Official, whom I hadn't visited in days.

'Ellie from England,' he said with an apparent attempt at politeness.

'Have you been in contact with Leyla's family?'

'Of course.'

'Did they know anything about her boyfriend?'

'I beg your pardon?'

'She had a boyfriend. Sounded as though it was quite new. He must be local — has he come forward?'

Karl chuckled, and I inched to punch him. 'I thought the serial killer was a woman? Did you now decide she has not risen from the dead?'

'New information has come to light and I have updated my investigation accordingly,' I said with a charming smile. 'That's how I was trained, at any rate.'

He gave me a look that suggested he'd quite like to squish me under his boot. 'What new information are you referring to?'

'Cissi Hallström,' I replied promptly.

'Who?'

'Cissi Hallström went missing a little over a year ago from the village at the other end of the forest. She too worked as a nanny, and she too had a new, charming boyfriend.'

Karl burst out laughing. 'Yes, I remember now. Have you been talking to the hysterical cousin? Cissi Hallström moved to Asia.'

'The *hysterical cousin* is concerned about her wellbeing. Isn't it your job to check?'

'Family business,' he shrugged scornfully.

'Is Leyla's death family business?'

Karl stopped short just before we reached the general store and glared at me. 'Leyla's family explained to me that she believed she was a witch. She read tarot cards, did spells and rituals at new moons, all that sort of nonsense. Aconite in minimal doses is considered a homoeopathic remedy for fear, anxiety, restlessness. It is a terrible tragedy that Leyla chose to drink what turned out to be a lethal dose. Please do not compound the tragedy with fairy stories about serial killers. Please respect her family's right to grieve in peace.' He gave me a dismissive smile, clearly having delivered his parting shot.

'Sorry, aren't her family in Azerbaijan?'

He frowned.

'So I'm not really affecting their peace by asking questions in Sweden, am I? It's not as though anyone else in the village is grieving. None of them even knew her from what I can gather. So what am I doing wrong, exactly?'

He didn't respond for a moment or two. The bonfire was reaching epic proportions, and it crossed my mind to wonder if it wasn't a bit close to the shop, but I supposed they knew what they were doing. A sudden grey cloud had descended, threatening rain. I should never have believed that brief promise of rain.

'Your time is yours to waste,' he said finally. 'I ask that you proceed with caution, remembering that just because you encountered a serial killer before, it does not increase your odds of finding one again. I ask that you respect the privacy and dignity of any relatives or friends you wish to approach, and that you truly consider whether your curiosity outweighs their peace. Finally, I ask that if you discover anything that suggests the people in this community are in danger, you bring such information to me before any publisher in London. I wish you all good luck.'

Biting down the compulsion to kick his pompous arse, I pasted my mile on one more time. 'You haven't answered my question.'

'Which question is that?'

'Did Leyla's boyfriend come forward?'

His hesitation was my answer.

'That's a bit odd, isn't it? It's a pretty tiny community and everyone has heard the news by now. He's not made himself known to you?'

'There is no reason he should. There is no investigation. He — if he exists — was not Leyla's next of kin.'

'But no one has mentioned him — like, *poor old Sven, this is hard on him, he was really falling for her*?' I pressed.

'No, nobody has said anything like that to me.'

He gave me a final nod and marched off, and I resisted sticking my tongue out behind his back, which I considered a win. The problem was he was right, I thought reluctantly. Or at least, he wasn't wrong. Cissi was apparently safe and well and living it up on some Thai beach, and Leyla may well have taken an accidental overdose of something she thought was safe.

But I couldn't ignore that prickling gut feeling. There was *something*, something I'd missed, something that made me uneasy, taunting me from the edge of my consciousness. Something Karl just said? Something Johan and I talked about last night?

I decided to treat myself to a latte before facing the hike up to the fancy house where Leyla had worked. I strolled towards the café deep in thought, barely noticing the usual cluster of ladies crowding the entrance. I don't really know what made me glance around as I opened the door, but I spotted Karl standing outside the general shop, reading something on his phone.

Something to do with Leyla? I wondered. Axel's mum, Pernilla came out of the shop, wiping her hands on her apron. As I watched, her face lit up at the sight of Karl and she approached him, arms wide, to envelope him in a hug.

Though I was across the road, her voice carried clearly. *Hur mår du, gubban?*

Gubban, I through. It translated literally as 'old man,' but was used affectionately for children, a bit as we would say 'little man,' to a small boy. Good friends might use it ironically from time to time, but an older adult using it to refer to a much younger one was likely to have known them since they were a child.

For some reason, that was when it clicked. Axel's girlfriend. I saw her, clearly, in my mind's eye, sitting proudly in the boat, watching him steer it into shore. A chill slithered down my spine as I realised what had been bothering me.

She was the absolute image of Tuva Hallström.

25

'They are identical twins,' Johan said quietly.

After Karl hopped into his car and drove off somewhere, I'd dawdled around the shop for as long as I could, hoping to engage Pernilla in casual conversation. No luck. I'd exchanged pleasantries with Pernilla a handful of times. She'd been at the St Lucia parade when Axel and I got chatting, and he'd introduced us then. She'd never been what you would call effusively friendly towards me, but she seemed to know that Axel and I were buddies and was willing to pass the time of day occasionally based on that. Today, however, she appeared to be deep in conversation or absorbed in stock take every time I casually wandered near her, so eventually, I gave up.

To keep up the fiction that I was shopping, I'd ended up buying half the shop. Johan's eyes widened comically as I started to unpack the gloriously random array of groceries, then his smile faded as I began to explain what I had seen in Axel's boat.

'I mean, Tuva and Axel could be seeing each other,' I said. I stuffed the three kinds of cheese and one chocolate pudding in the fridge and put the kettle on. 'That's perfectly possible. The singles scene around here must be slim pickings.'

'He has never told you his girlfriend's name?'

I shook my head. 'He's never mentioned her, truth be told. Which — I don't know now if it's weird or not. We're not exactly besties. We've just run in each other's company a couple of times, mostly in silence or chatting random nonsense. But I've mentioned you,' I added quickly. 'He knew you existed. I honestly can't remember now whether I had said your name or just *my boyfriend* or whatever.'

'So, him being together with Tuva is one possibility,' Johan said. 'Him being together with Cissi is another possibility. Linda said Tuva insisted Cissi could have met a man on the plane and taken off with him. She could have done the same thing before she got on the plane?'

'Even for someone who is rubbish at keeping in touch, living ten kilometres away from her sister with no contact in over a year is bizarre, isn't it?'

'I think so,' Johan shrugged. 'But I am not Tuva or Cissi.'

'I should ask Axel about her,' I said. 'I could go running with him and just ask him.'

Johan looked up, and I could see the concern in his eyes.

'Maybe not running,' I conceded with a rueful smile. I rubbed my arms. It was early to start the day's fire, but bugger it. I opened the glass door of the wood burner and started to brush out last night's ashes. 'I don't know if I think the idea of him being dangerous is ridiculous or not,' I said. 'I mean, what are we saying here? He kidnapped Cissi and has held her against her will for over a year? Why hold her for so long and then murder Leyla in a few days? She wasn't exactly trying to escape on the boat. Whoever she was, she looked quite happy there with him.'

I'd built a fire. It was a bit messy but it would do. I struck the match and watched as the little bits of kindling started to take alight. 'It is weird that he's never mentioned a girlfriend, not even said *we* do this or *our* plans for the weekend, the way most people do. It's nuts that his girlfriend may be considered missing by her family, if it is indeed Cissi. But —' I watched the fire start to crackle, then sighed helplessly. 'But I don't know what my gut is telling me about him.'

'Then forget your gut. Let's focus on evidence only. Come over here — I need to show you this.'

I followed Johan to the coffee table where printouts and handwritten notes were organised neatly. I skimmed over his notes on what we had discovered so far about Cissi, about Leyla, even about Tuva. There was a fourth pile, which I started to look through curiously.

Bahar Hameshi, an Iranian woman who ran a daycare, had gone missing just outside Kiruna in the Arctic Circle last October. Inga Holt, a primary teacher in Grisslehamn — maybe twenty minutes from here by car — disappeared just before Christmas. Maarji Ivanova, a Slovenian au pair, was reported missing by her employers just a few days ago. They lived in Norrtälje, a town less than an hour south of here on the way to Stockholm.

'You said you didn't think Leyla was the second,' he said grimly.

'But so many.' I shook my head.

'They all met a man they described as charming, or like from a fairy tale, in the days before they disappeared.'

'The one in Kiruna can't be connected, that's hours away.'

He shrugged. 'I know, it might be nothing. I came across a mention of Bahar in an article when I was trying to find out if any friend of Cissi's knew something about any man she was seeing before she left, and so I started searching further, and that's when I found Maarji.' He gazed at the pile helplessly. 'They might not all be connected at all, I just thought —'

'No bodies found other than Leyla?'

He shook his head.

'It is a lot of missing women in a small area in a short period,' I said. 'And Karl is still insisting that Leyla accidentally overdosed while doing something witchy..' I filled Johan in on my conversation with Karl.

'We don't know how far his area spreads,' Johan pointed out. 'He may not be aware of some of these others.'

'He knew exactly who I was talking about when I mentioned Cissi. And even if the others are in different jurisdictions, there are databases — it's the twenty-first century, for goodness sake. If he was taking Leyla's death remotely seriously, he would know. There is something else, too — I saw him with Pernilla, Axel's mum. They seemed close, maybe cousins or family friends.'

'Do you think that means he would cover up anything about Axel?'

'I'm not sure. It could be more that he wouldn't connect anything suspicious to Axel. What do they call it? Confirmation bias. He'll be primed to see his childhood friend or cousin or whatever they are as above suspicion.'

'We need to tread carefully,' Johan said. 'This is Axel's community. He has lived here all his life. They will be protective of him.'

My phone buzzed in my pocket and we both jumped a mile. It was Lena.

'Hey, sorry I only have a couple of minutes I'm heading into a meeting.'

I heard the roar of Stockholm traffic in the background

and felt oddly homesick for a moment. I put my phone on speaker so Johan could hear as well.

'I know you wanted to ask me something, but let me just fill you in on this first. I'm collaborating with Norrtälje police on a case at the moment, and when I was chatting with one of the detectives this morning I mentioned in passing I had been up in that area visiting friends recently.' The noise traffic stopped abruptly and Lena lowered her voice as she apparently entered a building. 'Do you know anything about the dead woman found in a church near your cottage earlier this week?'

'We do.'

I could hear Lena's smile. 'I thought you might. Well, I thought you should know that the forensic report just came back from the crime scene.'

My stomach gave a lurch and I scooted a tiny bit closer to Johan. The wind rattled through our rickety front door, and I suddenly wanted to jump up and jam the chair under the handle.

'The woman — Leyla — is not the first to have died there. They have found DNA traces of at least two other women who lay there before her.'

'Have they identified any of the other victims?' Johan asked.

'Not yet. They're running the DNA through the system, but it will be some hours at least.'

'We have some names to send you,' I said quietly.

26

I shrugged the hood of my jacket down as I stepped into the shop. The rain had started in the night, drumming on the roof of our tiny cottage as Johan and I lay wide awake. I'd jammed the chair under the front door handle before we went to bed, but every window felt flimsy and rickety.

I didn't even bother to pretend that Johan and I had eaten every scrap of the mountain I'd bought the day before and needed fresh supplies. I headed straight for the counter, where Pernilla stood deep in conversation with one of the ladies I recognised from the café crew. Neither of them acknowledged my arrival, but I'd played this game before and just stood, clearly waiting my turn, as they leisurely debated the merits of venison out of season.

'Hmm?' Pernilla finally turned to me, her cool blue eyes appraising as I gave her my most winning smile.

'Sorry to be a pain, but I've gone and deleted all my contacts doing something daft with my phone,' I grinned. 'So I've lost Axel's number — I promised him I'd text him about running.'

'Running?' She pursed her lips as though she had never heard of such a concept.

'We run together, now and then. We were supposed to go the other day but I got caught up in stuff and forgot to text him, so it's definitely up to me to organise the next one. I was hoping he might be kicking about — doesn't he help you with deliveries today?'

'He is busy today,' she said with a cold smile.

'Right, that's a shame. Would you mind terribly passing a message on?'

'What message?'

'Just — if you could let him know about my phone and ask him to text me.'

'If he wants to run with you?' she specified.

'Sure. Or, even if he doesn't, he could still shoot me a text so that I have his number again.'

'Hmm.' She nodded finally, as though there was no accounting for her son's taste. 'I will tell him.'

'Thank you so much.'

The rain had hardened into absolute sheets by the time I stepped back outside. I pulled my hood around my face as tightly as I could and sprinted across to the café. The owner brought a tray of biscuits out of the oven, and the whoosh of scent that filled the café made my knees wobble.

'I was going to have a hot chocolate, but now I've smelt the biscuits I'm going to need to eat one and is that too much chocolate?' I mused.

I was rewarded with a shy smile. 'Is there any such thing as too much chocolate?' he asked, and I nodded.

'You are absolutely correct, Sir. A hot chocolate and a chocolate chip biscuit, if you please. I'm Ellie, by the way,' I added as he started to froth the milk. 'I really should have said that before.'

'I am Tariq.'

'Very pleased to meet you, Tariq.'

Tariq's young assistant watched me shyly as he kneaded dough in the kitchen behind the counter. I gave him a smile but he turned away, mortified, so I decided to take my one win and leave him alone. I paid and headed to the same table where Johan and I had sat the other night. I'd give the rain a chance to recede back to drizzle at least before I ventured outside again. The double-chocolate fest hit the spot as I scrolled idly through social media, sprinkling the odd like here and there. Then it hit me — hadn't Axel sent me a friend request once upon a time?

I vaguely recalled having a quick peek out of mild nosiness when I first accepted him, and that there hadn't been anything of particular interest. Sure enough, I saw now that the most recent posts were a handful of *happy birthdays* from six months earlier. I screencapped a few quickly, then scrolled further. He didn't seem to post anything much himself. He'd shared an article about the library's opening last spring, and there were a couple of comments beneath offering congratulations. Last year's *happy birthdays*, and then — I stopped. I'd missed something.

Scrolling slowly back up his page, I spotted it.

'One more chocolate,' Tariq announced.

I looked up, startled, and he held out a small *chokladbol* on a saucer.

'It is a little misshapen so I can't sell it. Please — a gift.'

'That is so kind of you, thank you.' I forced a smile, though my heart was thudding in my ears. I took the chocolate ball covered in coconut shavings and bit into it as Tariq headed back to the counter. It was delicious.

I went to open my phone again. It took three tries for it to recognise my face, but finally the screen opened up and I tapped on the post. It was a photo, taken from a plane window, of landing in heavy snow. I could just see the familiar Scandinavian Airlines logo on the wing as it touched down on a runway covered in a thick layer of white. The caption read 'Welcome to winter!' and he had tagged the location.

Kiruna.

The date was last October. Axel Petersson was in Kiruna when Bahar disappeared.

THERE WAS A BREAK IN THE RAIN, THOUGH THE CLOUDS WERE still heavy and dark. I decided to make a run for it. I gathered my things and waved to Tariq, thanking him again for the *chokladbol*, then dashed out into the gloomy afternoon.

My burning lungs alerted me to the fact I was roaring along the road at a weird little trot, as though I needed the loo. I took a deep breath and slowed down, telling myself I was being ridiculous. I'd walked up and down this very road a hundred times before, at times much darker than this, and I'd never bothered to notice just how desolate it was.

He was stressed. When I saw him in the woods on Tuesday, I was nervous before recognising him because he looked angry. He was striding towards the church where Leyla's body would be found at any moment.

Cissi, Bahar, Inga, Leyla and Maarji. Five missing women, only one found. There had to be a reason.

What if Axel had been on his way to move Leyla to wherever the others ended up —

And I interrupted him?

Rain slicked trees rose overhead, dark and bare, barely discernible from their own shadows. There were a handful of cottages scattered around, plumes of smoke rising up here and there in the distance. I could see a truck parked just off the road up ahead, next to a pile of roughly chopped wood. It was one of those bizarrely giant ones you need a small stepladder to reach, gleaming black in the murky dusk. I couldn't see any sign of its driver, but felt slightly reassured at the sight of civilisation as I hurried past it.

Just another couple of hundred meters, I reminded myself. We'd get the fire on, and we would ban murder talk for one evening. Another cheesy movie or maybe a bit of delicious reality trash, and I'd tell Johan another ridiculous story from my absurd past.

Had I already told him about the time I appointed myself the bouncer of the gents' and arbitrarily refused random men access to pee? Every one of them meekly accepted my judgement, which I think said a lot more about their drunken confusion than my innate sense of authority, but I'd quite enjoyed the power trip all the same. Two or three headed for the ladies and the fourth solemnly asked my permission to go outside and piss on the street.

'Hello.'

Pure adrenaline shot through me and for a second I felt winded. 'Axel.'

He frowned, cocking his head to one side quizzically. 'Were you looking for me?'

27

'No — well, yeah, sorry —' I held up a hand as I tried to breathe like a normal person. 'I was — I was a million miles away there. Thinking about — ridiculous things.'

'But you are back here now, I hope?' he said. He was still staring at me with an intense, curious gaze, as though I were a specimen in a microscope. I glanced over his shoulder but I couldn't see any nearby lights. Hadn't our cottage been closer just a moment ago?

'Yes, I suppose so.' A light rain started to pitter-patter through the spindly branches overhead. 'Lucky me.'

'What were you thinking about?'

'I was thinking about the time I decided to be the bouncer of a men's toilet,' I replied honestly. *Act normal, keep chatting.* 'I'm still amazed none of them bopped me on the nose.'

'I am quite sure it is the rule that a man should never hit a woman.'

Axel smiled and suddenly looked like himself again. My

mate. My running buddy. A perfectly unremarkable, friendly neighbour.

'Ehh, I deserved it,' I grinned. 'I think there are exceptions to every rule. And yes, I did leave a message with your mum.' I wanted to take a step, to start strolling towards the cottage where Johan might glance out the window and see us, but Axel was blocking my path, and it is strangely difficult to just walk past someone.

'How annoying, losing all the numbers you had saved,' he shrugged. 'Though perhaps a good excuse not to text anyone you don't want to anymore?' He grinned, put on a terrible approximation of my London accent, 'I'm so sorry, I wanted to talk to you but I lost your number. Too bad, so sad.'

'Too bad, so sad?' I repeated. 'Where did you get that one from?'

'TV, I think. I like it. Too bad, so sad,' he sing-songed, and a little shiver of nerves danced down my spine. 'What a shame.'

'Anyway, we should definitely book in a running time soon — although, after the last couple of weeks, you're going to need to go slowly. I suspect I may have the lung capacity of an elderly smoker. I just knackered myself marching up the hill from the village.' I shook my head, fully aware I was jabbering like a budgie. 'Not impressive. Not even a little bit.'

'I think you are quite impressive, Ellie from England.'

'Well, you know, you're my pal,' I said, with a smile I'm fairly confident looked manic. 'You have to say that. Listen, that dinner we talked about the other night, we should organise it. Johan is genuinely a ridiculously amazing cook. I promise I would never invite you if it were me cooking, I wouldn't be that cruel, but he does all manner of impressive things with, I don't know, spices and whatnot. He can make asparagus taste good. And it would just be nice to have, like, a proper sit-down chat. We've not really done that yet, have we? So let's get it organised.'

I tried again to take a decisive step, but still, Axel didn't move so I was left standing uncomfortably close to him.

'That sounds like a very nice evening,' he said softly.

I drew back. The rain turned to sleet and I could feel the cold in my bones. The darkness was deep and unrelenting.

'Great, fab, let's get our diaries out. Though it's not as though we exactly have a glittering social life or anything, I'm pretty sure we could do any time that suited you — both of you, I mean,' I added awkwardly, regretting the words as soon as they were out my mouth. *Pick your time, Ellie.*

He frowned.

'Obviously your, girlfriend, or — wife? Both of you, are invited. Double date. It'll be great.'

'I don't have a girlfriend or a wife.'

'Oh. Sorry. I must have — I thought — I could have sworn, uhh, your mum mentioned — maybe I'm wrong. I must have misunderstood. Sorry. But — even better. More of Johan's lovely food for us.'

'I didn't know you had a boyfriend,' he said.

A weird feeling crunched in my stomach, guilt or fear or some noxious combination of the two. 'Oh, yeah, Johan. We've been together, gosh, a few years now. I still tell people it's new, or that I just moved here, but it's been a while now. Just over two years, I've lived in Sweden. Shocking that my Swedish isn't better, to be honest. Sorry, I thought — I could have sworn I mentioned — I suppose the misery of running distracts me from saying anything sensible.'

'I thought maybe you liked me,' he said with a soft,

embarrassed smile. Even in the darkness, I could sense his blush.

'Oh Axel — I, do like you. I mean, obviously — you're a brilliant guy, and you're so good looking,' I babbled like an absolute maniac. 'I'm sure any woman would — what a shit thing to say, sorry, forget that. I'm so sorry if I gave the wrong impression. I really hope we can still be mates.'

'Of course,' he said. 'We are always friends.'

'Oh good, I'm glad to hear that. Listen, if the idea of dinner seems weird, that's totally fine. We can stick to running. I just thought that maybe — I don't know. It would be nice.'

'It would be very nice.' He gave a rueful grin. 'I'll check my social diary.'

'Great. Fab. I'll look forward to it.'

The wind gave a particularly bitter gust, and I shivered.

'I should probably —' I began, and this time he stepped out my way.

'See you later, Ellie from England.'

28

Johan was asleep on the sofa when I got home. I covered him with the throw and stuck another log on the fire. My mind was whirring so fast I felt light-headed. What had happened out there? I grabbed a yoghurt for dinner with trembling hands and was just trying to extract a spoon from the drawer without waking Johan when my phone lit up with a call. Lena.

'Hi,' I whispered, closing the bedroom door behind me. 'Sorry, Johan is taking a nap.'

'Am I disturbing you?' she asked. I could hear a buzz of conversation behind her. I was reasonably sure she was at her desk at the police station on Kungsholmen.

'Not at all. It's good to hear your voice' I sat cross-legged on the bed and made a face at the unappetising yoghurt. 'I just got home —' I cut myself off, but Lena must have heard something in my voice.

'Did something happen?' she asked.

'No, not really — well. I don't know.' I hesitated a moment, trying to gather my thoughts. My heart was still racing and pins and needles danced at the tips of my fingers as I toyed with the foil yoghurt top. I hopped off the bed and pulled the blind down. I didn't want to see the darkness right now. 'You know the list of missing women Johan found?'

'Yes.'

'One of them, Cissi Hallström, has an identical twin sister. I visited the sister a few days ago. Then the following day, I spotted a friend of mine, well, acquaintance — this local guy I've run with a couple of times. He was in his boat, and there was a woman with him I was a bit surprised, mostly because he'd never mentioned a girlfriend, but then it hit me—

'Lena, I could have sworn she was Tuva's double. She and Cissi are identical twins. So then we started thinking that he — I don't know, he was holding her, that he could have killed the other women. He was in Kiruna when one of the other women went missing —' I sighed helplessly. 'But I ran into him, just now, and I — I just don't know. I honestly couldn't tell if I was frightened or felt sorry for him. It's mad that he was in Kiruna that week, but it's not conclusive, is it? It's quite touristy, isn't that where the Ice Hotel is?'

'Are you talking about Axel Pettersson?'

My heart fell to my toes. 'You know him?'

'I have read the name,' she said. I heard her tap a mousepad to wake her laptop up. 'He has been questioned since Maarji Ivanova went missing in Norrtälje earlier this month.'

'He has? Why?'

I heard her tap and could picture her scrolling through the notes on her tablet. 'He is an architect?'

'That's right.'

'The family that Maarji worked for are his clients. He is

designing an extension to their house. Their daughter reported thinking that Maarji had a new boyfriend, and the mother had previously thought possibly she had a little crush on Axel. Maarji had found reasons to be in the room when he was working, that sort of thing.

'So my friend at Norrtälje spoke with him, to find out how well they had known one another.' She broke off a moment as she read. 'Okay, so Axel said first that he had only ever spoken with Maarji in the home of her employers, but then later he admitted he once gave her a ride when he spotted her walking home at the side of the road. It was raining so he pulled in and offered to drive her the last few blocks as he was going there also. The daughter spotted them arriving together from her bedroom window. When asked, Axel said he had completely forgotten about the incident. According to his notes, my friend's impression is that was honest. It was quite a few weeks ago, and he seemed genuinely apologetic that he didn't remember. They do not intend on questioning him any further at this time. What do you think?'

'I'm not sure,' I said quietly. 'Without knowing who that woman in the boat is, it's all circumstantial, isn't it? He probably has dozens of architectural clients, and plenty of people go to stay at the Ice Hotel and see the Northern Lights. It could be something and nothing.'

'How close were you to them?'

'Not close. I was at the top of a hill looking down on them. I recognised him immediately, but — the more I think about her, the less I can even picture her face. I was so sure she looked exactly like Tuva, but all I really got is a glimpse of blonde hair. The more I think about it, the more I'm almost certain he mentioned a sister once.' I sighed. 'I might just be doubting my first impression — but I can't be sure.'

'There is one more thing,' Lena said. 'The lab has now confirmed that one set of DNA found at the church matches a sample given by Bahar Hashemi's relative.'

Ice dripped through my veins. 'The woman from Kiruna. She was in the church.'

'If you have evidence that Axel was in Kiruna around the time she disappeared, I need to tell my friend in Norrtälje. He will want to interview Axel again.'

'Of course,' I said faintly. 'It's on Axel's Facebook. He checked in as he was landing, three or four days before Bahar's friend reported her missing. Surely he wouldn't check in if he was going to —- find a victim?'

I could practically hear Lena shrugging down the phone. 'He may not have known at that point he would meet her, or he may have never considered anyone would connect her disappearance to his social media. Criminal masterminds who think of every angle to cover their tracks rarely exist outside of Superhero movies,' she added ruefully. 'Thank goodness.'

'There are no other DNA matches yet?'

'We are still trying to connect with close enough relatives to Maarji and Inga,' Lena said. 'But one DNA sample was from a Sami person, which Inga was, so pending confirmation I think that is likely to be a match also.'

'So there is still one unidentified set of DNA?'

'Which could be Cissi or Maarji.'

'Yes. Tuva refuses to give a sample to compare.'

'That doesn't seem terribly surprising having met her.'

Lena chuckled. 'I believe my colleagues are approaching Linda, the cousin, for a sample, so we may be able to confirm whether or not Cissi was in that church soon.'

I nodded, taking this in. 'Hold on a moment, did you say

there's only one unidentified sample?' I said. 'That means that either Cissi or Maarji could still be alive.'

'There is no way to be certain whether anyone was alive or dead when they shed the skin cells we found. Until we find and identify more bodies, any of them could still be alive.'

29

The big bonfire hadn't been lit yet, but several little fires in tin buckets had been set up around the clearing. Villagers milled around in the darkness, and there was a festive atmosphere, with hot cider being handed around and several raucous songs breaking out. Kids were tucked up in thick winter coats while hoards of skinny teenagers, seemingly impervious to the cold, roamed restlessly.

Despite the festive atmosphere, there was a tenseness, a sharp buzz of speculation dancing in the air. Police dog teams had been swarming through the forest all afternoon, searching for any sign of the missing women. They had been packing up, excited dogs piling into the backs of vans, when Johan and I passed on our way down to the village. They'd fallen silent as we approached, but Johan just caught the officer who seemed to be in charge, confirming they would widen the search area tomorrow.

'So they didn't find anything?' I murmured when we were out of earshot.

'Does not sound like it.'

I sighed and tucked my arm a bit tighter in his.

'Valborg is one of my favourite celebrations,' Johan said now as we strolled arm-in-arm through the crowd. A bit of a ragtag local choir appeared to be warming up in the far corner, and we were drawn inexorably towards what promised to be a lively assault on the ears. 'Partly because it's a mix up of a few different things and nobody cares. Some people say it heralded the beginning of the fertile summer season in the days when everybody was farmers. They gathered for one big celebration before working hard for the warm months to survive the winter. But also there is a pagan tradition that witches rise on the first of May, so we set fires to scare them away.'

I shivered. 'I like that,' I grinned. 'You've got a very sensible celebration to kick off the working season — but also, witches!'

'There are no witches if the fires work,' he laughed. Tariq's assistant, the skinny kid whose name I really should know, came by, handing out cider and mini cinnamon buns, which we gladly accepted.

'Excellent point.' I stood on tiptoe to kiss his cheek. Lena told me that the Norrtälje police were visiting Axel this afternoon, so Johan and I had decided we should take a break until we heard from her. I played hooky from work too, and we'd had a gorgeously contented day lying by the fire watching a couple of rubbish movies and chatting about nothing in particular. It had done us both the world of good. My mind was still whirring, but at a more manageable speed, like when a merry-go-round starts to slow at the end of a ride and you can discern individual horses and nauseous children.

Now, I caught myself peering through the crowd looking for him. I felt troubled and guilty, though I couldn't put my finger on why. If the circumstantial evidence was just that, then he would explain himself to the police, and that would be that. There was no way he would know I told them about him being in Kiruna.

I took the last bite of hot, spicy cinnamon bun and slipped my free hand into Johan's. The choir was just about to start. I spied Pernilla at the edge of the crowd. She looked furious, I thought, with a sinking feeling. She was scanning the crowd intently — looking for the guilty face of the person who turned her son in, no doubt. I snuggled under Johan's arm when she looked in my direction.

Despite their mismatching appearance, the choir harmonised beautifully. Traditional working songs about the joy of spring after the long winter filled the night air. It was chilly, but I was toasty warm between the fires, the cider and Johan.

When the choir finished to rapturous applause and a few whistles from me, the village, as one, sort of shuffled around to watch the lighting of the great bonfire. It was truly massive, I thought, the size of a small truck. We'd all be passing out from heatstroke as the night frost formed beyond the field.

I turned to say that to Johan when the first flames leapt into the sky, and the crowd gave an appreciative *ooooh*. The men in charge of lighting it — the exact sort of self-important middle-aged men in charge of such things the world over — drew back as the fire started to crackle.

Tariq waved as he passed by with a tray of fresh cinnamon buns, and when I spied Pernilla again, she was deep in conversation with a group of women, so perhaps not on the warpath after all.

Given how much rain and sleet we'd had, I was surprised at how well the fire was burning. Since moving to the cottage and taking charge of wood burner operations, I had become a bit of a self-appointed expert in the ways and means of fires. It didn't even seem to be sizzling and sparking as it might with damp wood but blazing merrily as the flames leapt higher and higher. The Bonfire Men in charge had covered it well with oily tarpaulins each night while they'd been building it, but you'd think some damp would have seeped in. To be fair to self-important middle-aged men, they did tend to know what they were doing.

I glanced over at Pernilla again, but she had melted into the crowd. My eye caught a blonde just turning away from me, and my stomach gave a twist. *Tuva?* From the general chat around the village, I knew that people came from miles around for this particular Valborg bonfire. One of the Bonfire Men had been bragging to Tariq about how *some people* referred to their fire as 'little Uppsala' — Uppsala being a big university town that held a famous Valborg celebration. Still, my heart thudded in my chest as I stood on tiptoe to scan the crowd for another glimpse of Tuva —

Or Cissi.

Then some kids towards the front started shouting, and a curious murmur ran through the crowd. I was too short to see over the sea of Swedes, but Johan was frowning.

'There is a Guy on the fire,' he said in surprise. 'Isn't that an English thing?'

He'd been horrified when I filled him on how, as children, we built a stuffed man from newspapers and old clothes then burned him to celebrate the burning and torture of a real person. It had never really occurred to me how gruesome it was, but now I thought about it, I was pretty sure they'd stopped burning an actual human effigy on Bonfire Night fires sometime over the last couple of decades.

'Maybe it's a local Valborg tradition? Burn the spirit of winter or something?' I grinned. 'Maybe it's meant to be Santa —'

But then I caught his expression, and my smile died.

'It is a person,' Johan whispered.

Then he was pushing his way through the crowd, his calm, authoritative voice announcing he was a nurse and to let him through. A stunned, horrified pall silenced the villagers as everyone obediently let him pass. I followed, my heart thudding in my ears. The people closest to the fire were screaming as a couple of the Bonfire Men clambered onto the fire as others tried to hold them back.

Cissi? I should have gone back to Tuva's today. What had I been *thinking* taking the day off when she was missing? *Or Maarji*? What if sending the police to Axel's had spooked him and —

The body had been pulled from the flames by the time we got to the front, water sizzling and snapping as the fire was doused and a horrifying smell of roasting meat filled the air. The clothes had melted, the flesh a charred, grotesque mess. Johan knelt by the body, leaning down to listen for any signs of breath in the chest, barking orders to call an ambulance.

It was a man. He was almost as tall as Johan. His white trainers were somehow more or less intact, touched only by a grey film of smoke. I stared at them intently, hollow, painful breaths wracking through me.

'He has been dead some hours,' Johan said quietly. 'There are signs of rigor mortis.'

I closed my eyes. It was a tiny mercy he hadn't burned to death before our eyes. Johan looked up at me, his eyes filled with horror and sympathy. 'I am so sorry, Ellie,' he said.

That was when I saw it was Axel.

30

xel. Axel. I kept thinking his name, but the word had lost all meaning.

The powerful roar of a red medical helicopter filled the air, a mighty wind whipping up debris from the fire as it slowly lowered through the clouds towards us. An icy rain had broken out, sweeping off the sea in freezing gusts. Nobody moved.

The officious middle-aged men had herded the crowd away from the clearing. Most of the young families had departed, parents gaily keeping up a steady stream of bright, inane chatter in the desperate hope their kids wouldn't realise what was going on. The rest of us had wandered, zombie-like, to the village street as a weird sense of mass shock settled through us all.

As the helicopter ground to stillness in the clearing, we stood in silence and uniformed paramedics leapt out. People in the crowd were looking from neighbour to neighbour, with pleading, intense eye contact, as though desperately hoping that someone, anyone, would confirm this was indeed a nightmare and that we'd all wake up at any moment. I could still feel the vibrations of the helicopter pulsing through me. I had a strange sensation that when my body realised the helicopter was still, I would collapse as though boneless.

Johan wrapped his arm firmly around my waist and I remembered that I wouldn't fall as long as he was there.

'Do you need to tell them anything?' I asked. My voice sounded somehow both shrill and robotic. I took a shaky breath and Johan held me closer.

'There is nothing to tell,' he said quietly. 'I had no possibility to save him, he was already long gone. It is better to let them just do their jobs.'

I nodded, my head feeling jerky and unfamiliar. 'The Norrtälje police were speaking to him this afternoon,' I whispered. 'They — someone will tell them?'

My words were swallowed by the wind as the ferocious thwack of the helicopter blades began to fill the air. The helicopter lifted slowly from the ground, listing to one side then the other. Though I knew a helicopter hardly needed a siren, there was something crushingly not urgent about its steady ascent. Finally, it was just a dot in the sky above, and the crowd seemed to let out a collective breath as though we had been released somehow.

A subdued murmur of chatter broke out. Tariq and his assistant emerged from the cafe with hot drinks and more buns, silently handing them out and refusing payment with a soft wave. People squeezed arms, shook heads, frowned at the sky as though expecting it to give them answers.

I accepted a cup from Tariq, my eyes filling with hot tears as I noticed that it was builders' tea. Johan had a black coffee. I tried to take a sip but my throat closed up.

'Do you think we should go home?' Johan said.

I started to nod, then I realised that this was the time

to find out if anyone knew anything. Like it or not, we were mixed up in this and we needed to see it through. My first crime section editor had drilled it into me that you always get to a scene as fast as humanly possible and not just to beat any other reporters. You get the real truth when people are still raw and stunned, he insisted. As hours slip by and the initial shock wears off, they have time to process, a chance for information to filter through even the mild agenda of what's not polite to say. Impressions and memories are never as pure again once anxiety and manners and loyalty and doubt twirl their way in. And that's assuming no one is deliberately hiding anything.

Sure enough, little hubs of conversation were starting to break out amongst the crowd. A couple of people broke down, crying into neighbours' shoulders, while still others seemed baffled, even indignant that the evening had taken such a turn. A handful of the teenagers were starting to get excited as reality faded and they realised what a splash it would make on social media. A few of them had whipped phones out and were recording the smouldering fire barricaded in by crime scene tape.

'What should we do?' Johan asked.

'We should — I think we should stay,' I said. 'These people knew Axel his entire life. This is the best time to find out — whatever there is to find out.' My horror didn't so much as fade as pack itself into a necessary box while my work brain took over. 'You take the lead,' I added. 'We shouldn't confuse matters with English. It's good if I can observe anyway. We should start with them —' I gestured towards the café ladies who were crowded around a friend who was drying her eyes and squeezing hands with a thankful smile. 'Give condolences, say something like, you didn't know Axel well but he seemed to be a great guy. See what they do with that.'

Johan nodded and obediently moved towards the group of women, but just then the crowd fell silent again. My breath caught in my throat as I caught sight of Pernilla. She was walking slowly, her face stoic but ashen, her eyes ravaged. The crowd parted for her, almost as though the force of her grief repelled them. Two women I vaguely recognised from around the village supported her. She leaned heavily on them as she staggered towards —

Me.

Me?

'What did you do?' she spat in English. Icy chills dashed over me. The force of the emotions rolling off her in waves was palpable; it washed over me, suffocating me.

'Me? I don't —'

'My son loved you. My beautiful child!'

'No — Pernilla, I'm so sorry —' My teeth were chattering, I didn't even know what words were coming out.

'It is too late to be sorry.'

'He didn't — I don't know what you are talking —'

'He loved you and you did this to him!' she screeched above the wind, her voice like nails on a blackboard.

'No — please, Pernilla, I am so, so sorry —'

'*Jag vet inte vad det här handlar om,*' Johan was saying, his soft authority giving me strength. '*Men Ellie* —'

'*Ellie älskade min son och han dog för henne!*' Pernilla screamed, her words ringing out over the crowd. I didn't catch it all, but I got *Ellie loved my son.* And he died — because of me? What was she talking about? What did that mean?

The crowd was staring at me with a mixture of disgust and fascination. It seemed as though they were moving closer, hemming me in. I wanted to back away. I wanted to fight my way through, to escape into fresh air where I could breathe freely. Johan's arm stayed firmly around my waist. It felt like about the only connection I had to sanity.

'*Jag är väldigt ledsen,*' Johan was saying quietly. '*Men vi måste diskutera detta en annan gång. Inte här, inte nu. Ellie och jag ska gå hem nu. Ursäkta,*' he turned to one of the bonfire men, who was staring agog. '*Låt oss förbi.*'

The man obediently stepped aside and Pernilla miraculously did not object as Johan firmly propelled me to the edge of crowd. We finally broke through to a blessedly empty road and I felt as though I could breathe again. Then I saw Karl waiting for us.

31

'I don't know. I don't know what she meant. I don't know how else to say it so that you understand. I could try to say it in Swedish?'

Karl's eyes hardened, and I knew I was on thin ice. I took a sip of water and tried to compose myself. We were in his office, a small building I'd never noticed before, tucked behind the library. I had no idea what time it was, I only knew I was dizzy with tiredness, words scrambling meaninglessly in my brain.

Johan was waiting in the tiny outer office. I could survive a night of no sleep, I thought, worry slithering around my guts. But it wasn't good for Johan. He needed rest. What if his heart —? I'd already asked Karl to tell Johan to go home, and he had refused. The only way I could make this end sooner was to tell Karl what he wanted to hear, but I couldn't do that.

'I hear from the Norrtälje police that a *local detective*, so to speak, gave them a list of missing women to investigate,' Karl said.

'Yes, that was me.'

I'd already admitted that, hours earlier. 'I told you this days ago. I am an investigative journalist. I have been looking into the case of missing women in this area. I've never kept that a secret. I've spoken to you about it more than once.'

Karl nodded and wrote something down. I glanced at his notebook, but I had zero hope of discerning the Swedish words in my current state of exhaustion, even if they had been right-side-up.

'And this *investigation* —' I could just hear the air quotation marks. 'Was coming to the conclusion that Axel Pettersson was a serial killer?'

I shook my head firmly. 'It was far from conclusive. Yes, I had found some circumstantial evidence suggesting he could be connected in some way. I was investigating further, but I had not yet reached any conclusions.'

'So you gave the name of a man you believed could be innocent to your contact at Stockholm police?'

'I didn't accuse him of anything. I discovered that he had visited Kiruna around the time Bahar Hameshi went missing. I passed that information on.'

'Axel went immediately from the airport to a two-week camping adventure in Abisko National Park,' Karl said. 'It is more than one hour north of Kiruna and one of the best places in the world to see the Aurora Borealis.'

'In that case, the detective will have excluded him from the enquiry.'

'He is excluded now,' Karl shot back.

'Yes, I suppose he is.'

A deep yawn overtook me and made my whole body shudder. I glanced at my empty coffee cup. I wanted to ask for more, but I was already on the edge of the jitters. 'Isn't that the normal way of things? You find out information, and you follow it up to determine if it is relevant? Are you suggesting I should have mentioned Axel to my contact in Stockholm only if I was already certain he was guilty? Surely that's not how the Swedish police operate?' I saw Karl's jaw tighten, and I felt a tiny dart of satisfaction.

'You gave his name to the police despite your — relationship?' he asked, and I would have punched him, if only I'd had the energy.

'I've told you a hundred times, Karl. If there was a lawyer here I suspect they would be pointing out this question has been asked and answered. There was no *relationship,* as you put it, between Axel and me. I have no idea where Pernilla got that from. We were friendly, but it was barely even a friendship — I can literally count on one hand the number of times we met.'

'But you have one another's phone numbers?'

'Yes, we swapped numbers. I've also got my elderly plumber's number and I'm not shagging him.' Was there such a thing as Tourettes but for sarky comments, I wondered. *Rein it in, Ellie.* Pissing Karl off wasn't going to get Johan home any time soon.

'Why did you exchange phone numbers with Axel Petersson?'

'We met running in the forest, a few months ago. The first or second week of January, I think. The snow was thick and it was almost full dark by mid afternoon. Axel and I turned onto the same path at the same time, and after a few minutes we ended up laughing about how awkward it was to be running silently side-by-side, each pretending the other wasn't there. I recognised him from the St Lucia parade at Christmas, so I introduced myself and we swapped numbers so that we could meet to be running buddies in the future.

Running is horrible, especially in the dark. It's nice to have company now and then.'

'So you were *running buddies*,' he said, stressing the phrase as though it was some universal code for bonking wildly in a forest in minus 10-degree weather.

'Even that is giving it more weight than it deserves. We've run together maybe three or four times, and said hello in the village on a handful of occasions.'

'In almost six months.'

'Like I said, I barely know the guy.'

'Hmm.' Karl sat back in his chair with a creak, scratched his stubble as he read over his notes.

'Look, he might have had a little crush,' I blurted. I regretted the words as soon as they were out my mouth, but my tongue seemed to have a mind of its own. If I gave him something, he might let us go. Right now, that was my only priority.

'How do you know that?'

I shrugged. 'The same way any of us can tell when someone is checking us out a bit. It was harmless. I'm not available so I hadn't given it much thought. But —'

Karl glanced up and I immediately looked away. I knew failing to meet his eye might make me look shifty, but I didn't care. 'I ran into him last night on my way home from the village. He — it kind of seemed as though he hadn't realised I had a boyfriend.'

'You kept your boyfriend a secret?'

'I didn't say that,' I snapped. 'I could have sworn I'd mentioned him, he normally crops up as I'm chatting, but like I say, Axel and I had not more than five or six conversations in the entire time we've known each other, so it's not that shocking he didn't know very much about my life.'

'Did he say that he was interested in you?'

'Not in so many words, but he — he said something like *I didn't know you had a boyfriend* in this sort of meaningful way, as though to convey he was disappointed I had a boyfriend without actually saying it. You know the way men talk in riddles when it comes to emotions and stuff?'

'No.'

'Well, they do. Not that it particularly matters because maybe Axel didn't even mean it in that way. I don't know. It's hardly relevant in any case, other than to possibly suggest how Pernilla got the wrong end of the stick about us. Maybe he told her he liked me and she misunderstood. Maybe he let her think it was mutual because he wanted it to be true. I've done that when I've had crushes in the past, made the story of an encounter seem a bit more than it was just to bask in that feeling of it maybe being true for a minute.' I was babbling but I couldn't seem to get the message to my mouth to stop.

'Or maybe she was just wildly acting out in the moments after discovering her son's death and I was there. Grief distorts everything. It makes you clutch at straws, makes everything seem ominous and deliberate when most of the time, people are just stumbling through life, barely noticing one another.

'What happened tonight — it doesn't bear thinking about. I can't begin to imagine what Pernilla is going through right now, and I have every sympathy for her. But if you are hoping to pin some fatal attraction affair on me, you are wasting your time. I've told you everything I know. And now, if you're not going to charge me with anything, I am going to go home.'

32

Despite my exhaustion at the police station, I was wide awake, gritty-eyed and queasy when the light started to trickle around the edge of our blinds. Johan was turned away from me, lying on his stomach. I couldn't tell whether he too was staring into space or if he had managed to drop off.

Did I believe what I had told Karl? Had Axel mentioned a little bit of interest in me to his mum and Pernilla put two and two together and made sixty-seven? I didn't know. It was the sort of thing my mum would do: before I met Johan, she had me married off to any Tom, Dick or Harry who looked in my direction. But Pernilla? Axel didn't strike me as the kind of guy who'd confide in his mum about a girl he fancied. A shudder tore through me and I rolled over, hugged my pillow tightly. It was abundantly clear that I didn't have the first idea of the kind of guy Axel was.

Had been. My breath caught in my throat as the sight of his broken and charred body reared up in my mind's eye. His face had barely been recognisable by the time Johan and I reached him. The flesh on his cheeks and neck had been almost curdled, melted into an agonising, bloody mess, but his profile was distinct, the outline of his body familiar.

And those white trainers. We'd talked about them. He ordered them online from the US: they were some brand you couldn't get in Sweden. I'd solemnly complimented him on his fancy taste in trainers, yet I'd stared at them for long minutes before recognition prickled in my brain.

He hadn't been placed on top of the fire, of course; he would have been spotted right away. He had been inside the top layer, as it were. The stack of wood was a good three metres, so he had been above the eye line of the Bonfire Men as they lit the fire and too camouflaged for anyone further back to spot in the dark. Until the logs around him had burnt away to reveal him.

I remembered going to the big bonfire on Wandsworth Common once with my mum. I must have been five or six, I was wearing my school duffel coat and it felt strange having it on over jeans and welly boots instead of the grey pinafore and tights of my school uniform. I spotted a few children from my school in the crowd, but none from my class. I hung around Mum, my hand firmly in hers, as she chatted to neighbours. The sparkler in my other hand had long since burnt out, but I didn't want to let it go because I was pretending in my head that it was a magic wand. Mum was laughing with some man — in retrospect, I suspect he was trying to chat her up and I was a tiny, grouchy cock blocker — and when the fire was light, he knelt down and explained to me the story of Guy Fawkes and why we burn a Guy on a bonfire. I already knew the story, we'd been talking about it all week at school, but I was too shy to interrupt him so I just nodded and tried to tune him out as flames leapt into the air and the Guy crumpled into glittering coals.

It was a coincidence that I was English and had grown

up waving sparklers at Guys on fires, I thought. Of course it was. I glanced at Johan's back. I wanted to say so out loud, to hear him agree, but he seemed to be fast asleep.

We'd had to wait in the police station as Karl interviewed each of the Bonfire Men. Two of them had been burnt badly enough to have been driven to the nearest hospital, but the remaining four sat, stunned and ashen, patiently waiting their turn. Karl left strict orders for us not to speak, which we of course ignored the moment he closed his office door.

The Bonfire Men had been setting the Valborg bonfire as a team for decades, they explained, and their fathers and uncles and grandfathers before them.

'You must have roots in our village to be given the honour of building the Valborg Bonfire,' one of them explained proudly. He looked shattered, so I decided that a lecture on inclusivity could wait. His eyes were unnaturally bright under a mask of smudged soot and he reminded me of the Dick Van Dyke character in *Mary Poppins*. The thought put me in mind of the ridiculous Julie Andrews voice I'd been doing to reassure myself when I ran into Axel in the forest, and I shuddered. It wasn't even a week ago, but it felt like a thousand years.

As I had suspected, the Bonfire Men knew their stuff when it came to bonfire construction. They spread a steel base on the grass below before building the foundations so that damp from the ground didn't rise and affect their masterpiece. The precise design, a sort of elaborate *Jenga*-like affair, had been established to ensure the perfect amount of airflow between logs to encourage steady, even burning.

'If there is too much air then the kindling burns itself out before it is hot enough for the bigger logs to take,' another Bonfire Man explained timidly. His eyes were wide and frightened and his hands were clasped tightly on his lap. 'If only that had happened tonight.' He closed his eyes with a deep, shuddery breath. I couldn't help but reach across to squeeze his hand.

'It wouldn't have saved Axel,' I said quietly.

He nodded, still trembling. He stared at me with wide, baffled eyes and I wasn't sure he had heard me.

'It must be someone who knew something of the principles of fire,' the first man said indignantly. 'To have rebuilt around him so carefully that none of us noticed anything amiss — I just don't understand it. We know everyone who —' He cut himself off with a sharp gasp, presumably realising the impact of his words.

'Has anyone new applied to join your group recently or asked about it?' I said suddenly. 'In the last year or so — or even just appeared a bit interested?'

They all exchanged worried looks then, one by one, shook their heads.

'Nobody applies to join our group,' the timid man said quietly. 'We build the Valborg fire.'

Now, I rolled onto my back and shoved the pillow away. A cobweb was drifting from the big light that we seldom switched on, and there was a hairline crack in the ceiling plaster snaking from the light fixture towards the doorframe. Johan was still silent, but I was no longer sure he was asleep.

The memory of Axel rushed at me from the shadows. *We got it wrong*, my mind whispered. According to Karl, Axel had an alibi for Bahar's disappearance. Lena hadn't returned my calls or texts so I didn't know how her friend's conversation with Axel had gone, but evidently, he hadn't arrested him. The events of the night certainly suggested the presence of another killer —

Unless they didn't.

Horror prickled over me like goosebumps as the thought formed in my mind. There were plenty of serial killers who chose death over facing the consequences of their actions. Was Axel one of them?

I thought about Leyla and the poisoned tea. There was no sign of any cup or flask in the church when she was found. She must have drunk the tea sometime earlier and then walked up to the church — or been forced or carried by her killer. Johan said that Axel was dead for several hours before the fire was set.

It would be almost impossible for someone to carry a guy of Axel's size onto that bonfire without destroying the whole thing. As the Bonfire Men explained it last night, the fire wasn't a solid structure but a carefully constructed house of cards. I remembered now how burning logs had tumbled away beneath the men's feet as they clambered wildly to try to drag Axel from the flames.

Once upon a time, I'd watched a Stockholm forensic team removing the body of a young man from the bench next to the Hammarby canal. He'd been a slip of a thing compared to Axel, but several people had struggled to lift him onto the stretcher. There's a reason they call it dead weight.

But could one person, having drunk a poisonous tea at home, climb up lightly enough not to leave a trace?

I knew a post mortem could reveal whether or not a body had been moved after death from the way that blood settled when the heart stopped pumping. I wondered if the burns Axel had suffered would affect that; his blood must have literally been boiling. Even if they could confirm he had climbed up there himself before any poison took hold, it didn't rule out his having done it under duress from the killer.

The other question was *when*. A dull headache tugged at my temples, but I knew any chance of sleep had long since passed. It must have been last night — or rather, the night before last. The far side of the bonfire wasn't easily visible from the village, but there must have been people milling around the clearing setting up for much of today. Johan said that rigor mortis had started to form before Axel was pulled from the fire. That meant he had been dead six to twelve hours, which fit with him having been on the fire since before dawn yesterday.

But *that* meant that Lena's friend couldn't have questioned him. It meant that by the time the detective from Norrtälje was knocking on Axel's door, he was already dead on the fire. Which made my theory of his choosing death over trial for murder less likely.

It was almost full light by the time Johan rolled over onto his back and rubbed his forehead with a yawn. I reached for his hand, but he didn't respond, leaving his arm lying heavy in the space between us. I turned on my side, gave him a searching look, but he stared at the ceiling.

'Why did you not tell me about your friendship with Axel?' he asked.

33

The first of May dawned cold and grey and every bit as chilly as April had been. My lungs complained as I hiked as fast as I could up the trail towards the church. I made a mental note to text Axel about a run this week. Then I remembered and ice dripped down my spine.

I'd been short with Johan that morning. I explained that I'd not mentioned Axel to him out of nothing but absent-mindedness, just as I'd told him the other day. Axel's death hadn't changed that.

'You tell me everything about your day, Ellie,' he said quietly. He was still in bed as I bustled about the bedroom, getting dressed with more force than was strictly necessary. The ridiculous excuse for a shower had done precisely nothing to improve my mood.

'I'll see you later,' I muttered, leaving him sitting there.

The stupid thing was, I was telling the truth. Mostly, at least. The very mild ego boost of Axel's possible interest was nothing; I'd have told Johan about that in a second.

Neither of us was a possessive partner. I'd had a wobble when I'd met Liv, the stunning ex he'd never mentioned, to be fair, but I think I was allowed a weak moment given the circumstances. When we first met in Thailand, we'd amused ourselves picking out people on the beach we reckoned the other would fancy. Johan's reaction to Axel in the shop the other night was exactly what I would have predicted. Amused, slightly proud, entirely unconcerned. We were far from a perfect couple, but we weren't *that* couple.

I hadn't told Johan about Axel because I felt guilty running with *anyone* when Johan could barely make it from one side of the cottage to the other without having to stop to catch his breath.

Once upon a time, Johan and I had worked out together. We'd done a power yoga class on the beach a week or two after we met. The sight of him holding a crow pose, sweat trickling between his powerful back muscles, had literally made me fall over with lust and I'd face-planted into a bolster. Not my most dignified moment, I grant you, but I owned it. After class, I'd whispered into his ear what really made me fall, and we'd — well, let's just say we made good use of our beach hut that day.

I'd kept quiet about running with Axel because of the cruelty of sharing something with someone else that I could no longer share with Johan. Which was why I could never explain why I didn't tell him. It was a right bloody, bastarding mess.

The church sat chilly and black against the silver-grey clouds. I stood at the edge of the clearing, just looking at it for a moment. I'd never really been one for believing in ghosts or spirits or energy. I'd got roped into a tarot night some friend-of-a-friend organised for her birthday once upon a time. I'd sat at the back, pissing myself laughing as the poor woman tried desperately to guess at whatever the person in front of her wanted to hear.

You're going to meet the love of your life very soon!
Umm, I've been married for a year.
Right, yes, but your love will take on a new and deeper level.
I'm pretty sure he's shagging his personal trainer.

Load of absolute bollocks. And yet now, standing in the shadow of the church, I could feel something that I couldn't quite articulate. I certainly wasn't expecting a headless spook to appear and start dancing around with jangling bones, but there was a tangible atmosphere. Something sat heavy in the icy air. The weight of the centuries the church had stood, perhaps, the lingering energy of generations upon generations celebrating and rejoicing and giving thanks.

I shuddered. I was getting fanciful in my old age, I thought crossly. I started to cross the dew-covered clearing towards the church itself then I stopped, uneasy suddenly. A memory prickled over me of being here with Axel.

It was our second run together, and I was a bit mortified at how tough I was finding tackling the hill while trying to keep pace with him. I'd paused in the clearing, pretending I was fascinated by the old church, while mostly trying to catch my breath before I hacked up a lung. I'd asked him about the church, and he told me how old it was, how it was built on an even older site of pagan worship.

I muttered some daft joke about hoping there was Viking treasure for the taking and he laughed and said —

Damnit, what did he say? The memory flittered at the edge of my consciousness. I could see him, towering over me, barely breaking a sweat.

He had an odd laugh. It was loud, a *shout* of laughter that seemed joyful, yet now I thought about it, didn't contain any real mirth. It was like a performance of laughter.

When Johan laughed, he giggled like a child. High-pitched, red-faced, it rendered him an absolute mess of a human. It was impossible not to join in, even if I had no idea what had set him off.

That day, here in this clearing, Axel gave a shout of laughter, and he said —

It's not Viking treasure you'll find in there.

My breath grew hard and sharp in my chest and I grabbed a nearby tree for support. It was slick and icy-cold and I regretted it immediately, but I didn't let go. *It's not Viking treasure you'll find in there.*

I hadn't given it a moment's thought. I supposed it was an odd thing to say, but at the time I'd been more concerned with the growing stitch in my side and whether I'd survive keeping pace with him the rest of the way. I'd sort of chuckled politely, then asked if we should crack on. He nodded and we'd finished our run and I'd clean forgotten the entire exchange.

It's not Viking treasure you'll find in there.

What would I find in there, Axel?

I grit my teeth as I climbed up the crumbling steps. It wasn't even particularly windy today, yet there was still a shrill whistle echoing around the ancient stones. I forced myself to cross the threshold, and the temperature plummeted immediately. Lena had said something about how the old stones' chill had helped preserve the trace DNA found on the altar for longer than usual.

Was that what Axel meant that day? Had he been telling me that I wouldn't find Viking treasure, but the remains of his victims? Had he been sounding me out, seeing how I would react before telling me more? Had I ignored a serial killer's confession because I was more concerned with walking off a stitch?

I'd done enough research on serial killers to know that

keeping their activities secret was difficult for them. They ached to tease, to brag, to watch the horror dawn in another person's eyes as they grasped what they were hearing. Mia was a rare exception to that. She had enjoyed her double life, exalted in her secret that allowed her to live her sick version of the best of both worlds.

Every single cell in my body screamed at me to turn, to run far away from the church as I walked slowly up the aisle. I remembered my daft thought about being a forced demon bride and forced a laugh. A sharp laugh that echoed horribly around the cloying silence.

'*Ursäkta?*'

I whirled around, my scream caught in my throat. A couple stood where the doorway would have been, peering at me curiously. In her fifties or so, sensible hiking gear. After a moment I realised the woman was one of the café gang. She blinked as she recognised me.

'Ellie?' she said hesitantly.

'Hi,' I breathed, a blush creeping over me as I realised they must have heard my laughter and came in here to find me chuckling my way up the aisle to an invisible demon groom. The day after being accused of an affair with a man who had ended up on the village bonfire. I really knew how to get in with the neighbours. 'Sorry,' I muttered quickly, 'I was just —'

'This structure is not safe.' Her eyes fell on the crime scene tape still guarding the alter. 'You should not be here.'

'I know, I'm sorry. I was just —'

'We have petitioned the commune to build a fence around the church since many years,' the man added. 'Many young people come here to drink and party, and parts of the walls could fall at any time.'

'Who comes here?'

'Excuse me?'

'Do you know any teenagers who have come here this winter?' They both stared at me blankly, but I persevered. 'This is a crime scene. They might have seen something they don't realise is significant. I'd like to speak to them.'

'Do you work with the police, Ellie?' the woman asked, politely as disapproval flickered in her eyes.

'I'm a journalist,' I said. 'Freedom of press, and all that.'

'Yes, the media has much to answer for,' she said mildly.

'I'll ask around about the teenagers,' I said firmly. 'If they have any information that might help us understand the terrible things that have happened here, it is their civic duty to come forward.'

34

I refused to meet any of the silent, curious stares that followed me through the village as I walked as quickly as I could from one end to the other. Only Tariq, wiping tables outside his café, gave me a small friendly smile as I passed.

Drizzle turned to sleet, then light snow as I headed up the other hill to the fancy house. My legs burned and my knee randomly ached for no good reason. Also, I was hungry for good measure. *The bloody family better be bloody home,* I told myself grimly as the imposing structure came into view.

There was no car in the drive.

I sighed furiously, climbed the front steps anyway and banged noisily on the door. Where were these damned people? What on earth were they finding to keep them so occupied in this godforsaken, arse-end-of-beyond village? I thumped again. There was only silence from within. No TV on in the den, no footsteps, no *muu-uum, there's someone at the door.*

In a move that was by now well-practised, I clambered

over the wooden railing onto the deck. The snow was starting to settle, giving the sun loungers and gigantic barbecue an icing-sugar dusting. I skidded on a little patch of ice and yanked my sore knee as I righted myself.

'It's bloody May!' I shouted at the snow, but oddly enough, it paid me no heed.

Cupping my hands against the glass, I peered into the luxurious kitchen-lounge. There was a thick Arran throw tossed over the sofa that hadn't been there the last time I looked and a hardback book on the coffee table. The bread and butter had been tidied away, but a pot sat on the stove, a wooden spoon sticking out of it. An open tin on the counter looked like soup, and clothes were piled on one of the stools tucked under the breakfast bar.

I narrowed my eyes, taking in the scene. Something had caught my eye but I didn't know what. It was pretty standard family messiness. I guessed the young teenager I'd talked to had heated himself some soup while his mum read on the sofa. Maybe she asked him to take the pile of laundry up to his room, but then for some reason, they'd all gone out, again, without tidying up.

Clambering off the deck, I wandered over to the garage where Leyla lived. Crossing my fingers briefly that this wouldn't be the moment they finally decided to come home, I ran up the steps to the small first-floor landing. There was, annoyingly, no window in the door as I'd hoped, and a quick lean over the railing confirmed I'd need to be Spider-Man to peek in any of the other windows. I stood on the landing a moment, looking out over the treetops and the tiny hint of grey water far below, then impulsively tried the door handle.

It opened. I was so startled I nearly jumped back as the door swung inwards to reveal a shadowy hallway. I hesitated, every instinct sternly telling me I had absolutely no right to enter the murdered woman's home and that the family could come home at any minute. Then I stepped inside.

Beyond the little entrance hallway, the flat was an airy, open-plan studio. Large picture windows let in light and a stunning view of the forest and sea. It was furnished blandly, functionally, IKEA basic range all the way. A beige sofa in a kind of canvas fabric, fake wood coffee table, little round kitchen table and blue kitchen shelves containing neat rows of mason jars of pasta and legumes. A quick peek in the kitchen cabinet revealed four identical blue mugs, matching plates and cereal bowls, four glasses. They were all uniformly lined up on the shelf like a display in a shop, as opposed to the higgledy-piggledy mess our kitchen cupboard became whenever it was my turn to unload the dishwasher.

Tucked behind the kitchen was a little sleeping nook with a futon, a few empty shelves, a clothes rail, and a door I guessed led to a bathroom. Blue and white linen sat folded neatly on the bare mattress. There were absolutely no personal effects. No photos, no handmade throw cushions in bright colours, no favourite mug.

No clothes, either. Clearly, Leyla's things had been packed up and presumably sent to her family. I wished I could have seen the apartment before. It was impossible to tell now if it had felt lived-in and homey with her personal knickknacks scattered around, or if she had actually lived in this stark, utilitarian style.

There wasn't anything I could learn about Leyla in here, I decided reluctantly. Other than confirmation that none of the house windows looked directly into the flat. She may have had to eat off identical plates every night of the week, but at least she could do so in private, I thought as I made my way back to the door.

The hallway didn't get any direct light when the door was closed, so it wasn't until I opened the door to leave that I spotted my footprint on the beige rug. *Shit.* I crouched on the floor and gingerly flicked at the mud. It was dry, so I was able to dust the worst of it off, but the only way I'd get rid of it altogether would be with a damp cloth — and if I left the cloth out to dry it would be just as much of a giveaway someone had been here as the footprint. *Shit.*

Maybe I could come back with a cloth from home? I glanced at my watch and calculated how long it would take me to jog home and back again. It would be dinner time by the time I returned. Surely the family would be home by then. Even though they couldn't see the flat easily from the house, it was too much of a risk. Maybe a trace of a muddy footprint wasn't the end of the world, I thought. Possibly whoever had carried Leyla's suitcases would assume it was them.

Or could I turn the rug over? It would mean the label being right side up, but maybe I could tuck it under, and either way, it shouldn't be too noticeable. Surely no one would jump to nefarious — albeit correct — conclusions upon noticing an upturned label.

I lifted the corner closest to me and immediately spotted the photograph that had slipped underneath. It was the kind that prints straight from the camera. My mum had that sort of camera when I was little. I remembered the anticipation of waiting for it to develop, watching enthralled as I appeared first as a shadow then as a slightly blurry person, and finally, recognisably me.

Leyla smiled out from the past and sadness settled over me. She looked like fun, like someone I would love to be friends with. In the photo that had appeared in the local newspaper, she looked solemn, almost a bit sullen. But this photo seemed to have caught her mid-laugh. Her face lit up with happiness. She was snuggled with a man who rested his cheek on the top of her head, holding her close. His smile was a bit more contained but no less joyful. Her arms were wrapped around one of his, pulling him as close as she possibly could. There was absolutely no question that this was a couple, and one very much in love at that.

    The man was not Axel.

35

'I am so sorry, the café is now closed,' Tariq smiled with kind eyes as he opened the door. I'd been battering on it for several seconds, so his polite greeting was significantly more than I deserved.

'I know, I am sorry to disturb you, honestly — it's just that —'

'It is okay, Ellie.' He stepped aside to let me in, and I was hit by a welcome blast of warmth and the smell of sweet spices. Tramping around forests all day had left me almost numb to the cold, but my skin now prickled back to life and I felt instantly cheered.

'Do you need some tea?' Tariq asked. 'Or perhaps a hot chocolate?'

'That is so kind of you, Tariq, but I'm not here to bother you as a customer, I promise. Your assistant — is he still here?'

Something clouded in Tariq's eyes and he hesitated.

'I'm not going to cause any trouble, I promise. I won't report anything he says to the police or any authority, I just need to speak with him, if that is okay.'

Tariq considered a moment, then gave a small nod. 'I will ask him. If he says no, I must ask you to leave.'

'I understand completely.'

He went into the back, and I sat at my usual table. They hadn't cleared the candles away yet, and I was grateful for the tiny cheery flicker as I waited. After a few moments, the quiet young man took the seat opposite me, and Tariq pulled up a chair from the next table.

'He asked that I stay with him.'

'Of course,' I smiled at the young man. 'That is absolutely fine.'

'This is Kadin,' Tariq said.

I smiled. 'I'm Ellie. I'm very pleased to meet you. Thank you for speaking to me.'

Kadin nodded shyly. I reached into my pocket and pulled out the photograph. Both men looked at it, then Kadin's face crumpled into tears. Tariq rubbed Kadin's arm as he swallowed down a sob.

'I am so sorry,' I said quietly. 'I spoke to the young boy Leyla took care of, and he told me a little bit about her. She sounded like a wonderful person.'

'Yes,' Kadin mumbled. He took a shaky breath. He hadn't taken his eyes off the photo.

'You were in a relationship?' He glanced to Tariq for reassurance, and Tariq nodded.

'Yes, we were.' He stared at the image of Leyla laughing, a fat tear rolling unheeded down his cheek. 'Her employers did not like her to have —' he hesitated, searching for the English word. 'Her own life? They were very — like teachers?'

'Strict?'

'Yes. Leyla cared very much for the little boy, but it was not a happy family. Leyla and I were saving up so we could afford our own home, maybe back in our country.' He stopped again, and Tariq squeezed his shoulder.

'We can trust Ellie,' he said, and I shot him a grateful smile.

'We have not permissions to be in Sweden,' Kadin admitted, his eyes fearful.

I nodded.

'We try, but our country is not in EU, so —'

'I know how that feels,' I grinned cynically and was rewarded with a small smile.

'That is why I do not tell the policeman about me and Leyla. He maybe ask to see my visa and make trouble for Tariq. I have nothing to tell him anyway.' Kadin's eyes filled up again and he fought down a sob. 'I do not know what happened to her.'

'Was she interested in magic?' I asked.

'Magic?' he stared in alarm.

'Witchy things, spells, tarot cards maybe.'

'No,' he said firmly. 'Nothing like that.'

'Alternative medicine? Herbal portions or remedies with healing properties?'

He shook his head in horror. 'She would only take medicine from doctor to heal. We have real doctors in our country.'

'Of course, I'm so sorry — I didn't mean to imply you didn't. There was a reason for the question, I promise.'

He nodded.

'Did she have any other friends in the area? Any girlfriends? Maybe another au pair?'

'No. She only worked and saw me. She was very fond of the little boy, Fritjof. He thought he was too old for babysitter so they said they were friends.'

I smiled. 'He told me that too.'

'She was very kind person.' He took a shuddery breath. Tariq got up and returned to the table with three rich, oozy brownies. My stomach growled but I wasn't sure if it was fair to munch chocolate while questioning Kadin about the death of the woman he loved. Luckily, he grabbed one and tore in, so I felt I could too. The sugar hit my bloodstream almost immediately and I felt about eighty-five thousand times more alive.

'When was the last time you saw Leyla?'

'Two days before —' his voice cracked and I nodded quickly. He didn't have to say it. 'We argued a little. I thought we should pause our relationship so she could keep her job until we had enough money, but she felt it was not fair of her employers to demand she exist only to work for them. I understood her feeling, but I thought just a few weeks would not matter, we had our whole lives to spend together.'

He sighed and took another bite of brownie. 'Leyla was very strong in her opinions, so she told me I was weak and not courageous and she went back to her apartment.' He chuckled. 'She did this many times in our relationship, I was not so worried.

'We planned to meet again two days later. I was going to tell her then I understood her opinion and was willing to continue our relationship despite what her employers thought. She was right, I had been afraid, but you cannot live a life afraid. When she did not show up, I thought maybe she had decided she understood my opinion and was going to stay with her job. I did not worry, until —' He took a ragged breath, his hand trembling as he toyed with the last bit of brownie.

'The night you planned to meet, when she didn't show up, that was Saturday?' I said.

'Yes.'

'According to the little boy, that was the day she was fired. She left their house that night, but she didn't come and meet you. Someone must have intercepted her, maybe offered to help her.'

I thought of Axel half-carrying me home two days later.

'Someone she trusted,' Tariq said.

I shrugged. 'Some people are very good at creating trust right away. There was a case years ago, in the States, of a serial killer who dressed up as a policeman to offer lifts to women.'

'She would not go with a policeman,' Kadin said firmly. 'She did not like police. She did not like many men at all,' he added with a sad smile. 'Only me.'

36

Tariq offered me a lift home, but I could see they still had work to do, and the walk would help clear my head. I was so deep in thought, in fact, that I was nearly at our cottage before I knew it. The clouds had lifted, and stars twinkled overhead.

I stopped for a moment to enjoy the sight. This was one thing you never got to see in a city, I thought. There was a cluster of stars just above me that I was almost sure was some kind of famous constellation, but I wasn't educated enough to be able to identify it. Johan would know, I thought, with a rush of affection. He always knew that sort of thing.

My head was spinning. There were so many disparate strands of information that stubbornly refused to form any kind of cohesive picture. There was a quotation I remember reading, at uni or something, from some famous sculptor. He was asked how he sculpts something-or-other, a horse, let's say. He responded that he took a lump of clay and removed everything that wasn't a horse.

I often felt that an investigation could be a bit like that.

At the beginning of the case, you're faced with a mountain of information. Facts about the victim's or victims' lives, their movements leading to their death, not to mention a myriad of other things that happened in the vicinity of where they died. The trick is to work through this mass of facts until you remove everything relevant to the investigation. Then you follow the threads that remain until, hey presto, the crime is solved.

In theory, anyway.

But I felt in a hopeless fog with this one. The information had only just barely started to form into some kind of sense when Axel's death threw it back into disarray. He had an alibi for Bahar's disappearance, and he wasn't Leyla's boyfriend. He had been in the forest when Leyla was discovered at the church, but then so had I.

A dull headache thudded behind my eyes, which was part-cold, part-hunger and part the utter frustration of uselessness. The lights of our cottage came into view, and I realised that I could fix two of those things shortly, albeit only two. My phone buzzed in my pocket. It was an unknown number.

'Hello?'

'Yes, hello, do you want to speak English?' a woman's voice, clipped and officious but pleasant, asked.

'Umm, yes, if that is alright — who am I speaking to please?'

'My name is Elin Nilsson. My au pair is Maarji Ivanova. I was given a message you wanted to speak with me.'

'Yes, hi. Thank you so much for phoning. I take it you haven't heard anything from Maarji yet?'

'No.' I heard the note of genuine sorrow in Elin's voice, could almost see her sad smile. In the background, I could hear a kids' show blaring on the TV and a child giggling over the laughtrack. I sensed it was a warm home.

'I'm so sorry,' I said.

'Is it true Axel is dead?' she asked. 'He seemed like such a kind man.'

'Did you know him well?'

'No, not terribly. He worked on the designs for our extension for some months. My husband and I couldn't agree on what we wanted, and Axel was so patient with us, updating and updating the designs so many times. On a few occasions, if it was quite late when our meeting ended, we asked him to join us for dinner.' She chuckled. 'He always seemed a little bit terrified of the chaos of our home.'

'Did Maarji seem interested in him to you?' I asked. 'Like a crush or something?'

'My daughter thought so, but she is at an age where she is convinced everyone is in love. My brother and I have quite similar dogs who love to play together, and my daughter regularly announces they want to get married. To be honest, I thought Axel was quite attractive. My husband teased me about it a few times. But I am fairly sure he seemed like an old man to Maarji. She is only in her early twenties.'

Like Leyla, I thought. 'And your daughter said she had a boyfriend?'

I could sense Elin shrugging. 'I'm not sure if it was boyfriend or friend with benefits or what do you say. All these terms they have these days, talking stage and ghosting and situationship, it all seems much too complicated to me. But yes, there was a young man Maarji seemed to be rather taken with, whatever that means.'

'And you don't think it was Axel?'

'No, definitely not. My daughter met this young man when she and Maarji were out walking in the park. My daughter's description was a little confusing, but I think she is describing a gardener for the city. She said he had a little car he could drive on the grass, and I guess she means the carts for clippings and things. She said that Maarji stopped to talk with him for a while, but she did not know his name.'

'I guess the police have spoken to his employers?'

'Yes, but as I say, my daughter is six, her descriptions are perhaps not so helpful. They have not managed to identify or speak to this boy. For what it is worth, I did not like this boy. I have told the police this. He was my first thought when we realised she was missing, but now I understand there are several missing women, so perhaps he is just not nice.'

'In what way didn't you like him?'

'I don't know if he is a bad person or just immature and a little too entitled, but I —' she laughed ruefully. 'Once upon a time, I liked bad boys. I fell for all those lines about how I was the only one who understood him, that we were something special together but that I should not expect too much from him because the pressure to be a decent human being made his cock sad or some such bullshit.'

'Sounds familiar,' I laughed. I liked Elin Nilsson.

'I tried to gently suggest to Maarji that he was manipulative and perhaps not worth her time, but she was not ready to hear it yet.' Elin gave a shaky sigh, I could hear the tears dancing in her voice. 'I hope she will get the opportunity to outgrow men like that.'

37

I hung up. Exhaustion settled in my bones as I trudged the last few steps towards our cottage. Johan was sitting outside, I noted with surprise. There was a creaky wooden swing hanging from the front porch. We joked when we first moved in that we were entirely too young and fabulous to be spending our evenings watching the sunset from that swing, but that we would probably do it anyway.

'Aren't you freezing?' I called.

He was wrapped up in his Arctic jacket, the swing screeching softly as he rocked back and forth. He looked up at me, and my heart fell into my toes.

'What's going on?' I hurried over the last few metres of frosty mud. 'Has something happened?'

'You didn't answer my question, Ellie,' he said quietly.

'What question? What are you talking about?'

'Why didn't you tell me about Axel?'

My stomach gave a twist. 'I've told you already. Because there was nothing to tell, Johan. He and I met up not more than a handful of times, and every time I got home, you would be asleep, or —'

'Ahh.' His voice was cold. 'I was too sick to understand your new friendship.'

'That's not fair, I didn't say that. I'm literally telling you what happened — by the time you got up I was no longer thinking about my run, because running is horrible and I try to forget it as soon as possible.'

'Okay,' he nodded tightly. He got up and steadied himself against the porch beam. 'Forget it.'

'No, hold on a minute, not okay, and we're not going to forget it — you can't come at me with an accusation like that, making out like I was keeping some big secret from you and then just drop it. If you're accusing me of something, then come out with it properly and we'll talk about it.'

'I just —'

'You just what? You *just* think I was randomly shagging Axel? After everything we've been through, you're now telling me that you believe Pernilla and Karl over me ? That's what's happening right now, is it, Johan?'

'Of course not, Ellie, I didn't say —'

'So what are you —?'

'What do you want me to say?' he snapped. 'Did you keep the secret from me or didn't you?'

'Forgetting to mention something isn't the same as keeping a secret!' Rage pulsed through me and my face felt hot despite the icy night.

'You didn't want me to know about the strong man with the working heart who could run alongside you.'

Fuck, he knew. He slammed the door behind him. I flung it open and followed him inside, letting it slam behind me.

'Johan, it's not your fault that you are —'

'An invalid.'

'Yes! So what? You are ill. You nearly died and it is taking you a long time to recover and that is entirely understandable and natural, but it's —'

'What?'

'It's not been that easy. It's been lonely and scary, and how can I turn to you when it's you that I'm worried about? I've tried to do everything right, be the supportive girlfriend, but I don't know how — I don't know what I'm doing here.'

'I did not receive training on how to live with a malfunctioning heart either.'

'I know! That's exactly why I didn't want to burden you with my stupid worries. But getting to casually pass the time of day with an acquaintance during a run was —' I sighed, searching for the right word, knowing it would be the wrong one. 'It was an escape. I felt horrible that it was something you couldn't join in with, so yeah, I just kept it to myself rather than risk making you feel shit. I'm sorry.'

'Okay,' he said again. He turned away from me, but now we'd started, we were bloody well going to finish it.

'Johan, you're not being fair. In any normal relationship, we would expect to have colleagues and gym buddies and *lives* outside of each other. You think Maddie and Lena know every single last detail about each other's days? Maddie watches reality TV on her phone during her lunch break because Lena will give her a hard time about it not being the kind of pretentious artsy-fartsy stuff Lena likes. Do you think that's some great betrayal that means they are lying together? The two of us exist in this little bubble where it's just the two of us and we only have each other and —'

'Because all my friends are dead!'

His voice resounded around the tiny cottage. He

clutched the counter for support, breathing heavily, his face turning alarmingly red. My heart leapt into my mouth.

'Johan, please calm down, you need to breathe —'

'I knew Krister more than thirty years,' he said, his voice ragged and laboured. 'He was my brother, my support though my father's death, my mother's drinking. He was there when I began to understand that Liv was not in love with me and I was completely alone in the world. But I wasn't alone — Krister was there. He was my family. Closer than Liv, closer than Mia. Now he's gone and we never talk about him. When Liv died, I grieved for her. Friends, all those people who loved her, got in touch to sympathise, remember her, and pay tribute to her. But Krister? It was silence.

'Nobody wanted to break my heart while my heart was actually broken. I didn't even see him in those last moments. I was unconscious when he needed me.'

He took a shaky breath as the wave of anger burned out. 'It is cruel that you are the only person left that I love. It is too much to ask of you, too much for you to take —'

'It's not —' I burst into tears as I ran to him. I hopped onto the breakfast bar so that I could gather him into my arms, hold him close. 'It's not too much,' I whispered fiercely into his hair. I could feel his pulse racing and it made me want to scream with terror. He had to be okay. 'It's exactly the right amount. I promise. Please believe me, Johan. I can take this and anything else this bloody bastard fucking universe throws at us. I am stronger than you think.'

He took my face in his hands and kissed my nose, then leaned his forehead against mine. We were silent for a few moments, listening to one another breathe. Gradually his heart rate stopped leaping around like popcorn and cool relief trickled through me.

'You are as strong as I think,' he murmured. 'And that is so crazy strong. I'm sorry I should not have —'

'Don't apologise.' I kissed him. 'You don't need to. It was stupid of me to never mention my running buddy. But it was just that. Thoughtless. Daft. I thought I was protecting you but it was stupid and I am so sorry.'

'I know,' he said with a sigh, kissing me again. He pulled me closer and I wrapped my legs around his waist as we kissed. 'I have been just sitting here all day feeling so useless that I started to think and —' he murmured between kisses.

'Well that was your first mistake,' I grinned. He ran his hand up my back, under my jumper and I shivered. 'We'll have none of that thinking nonsense.' His fingers found my bra strap and I gasped and then our fight was very much over.

38

The warmth made the tips of Maarji's finger sting and she wanted to cry. Just one sip. One sip wouldn't kill her.

But one sip could make her very ill and she couldn't afford that. She clutched the cup, closed her eyes, willing the warmth to flood through her body. She tried holding it closer, hugging it like a hot water bottle, but she only succeeded in spilling some of the liquid onto her top, where it instantly cooled.

With trembling hands, she put the cup on the floor. If she held it much longer, she wouldn't be able to stop herself gulping the whole lot down. The comfort of the warmth spreading through her would be quickly followed by nausea and stomach pains, and then the tingling and numbness would begin.

And not long after that her heart would stop.

Maarji didn't have half the brains her sister did, but she sometimes helped out in Alina's chemist shop after school. Maarji liked serving customers and enjoyed it when they gossiped or poured out their troubles. Even though Alina made her explain that she wasn't the pharmacist and couldn't give them any medical advice, most of them continued to chat away about their dizzy spells or *ingrown toenails. Maarji happily listened and made sympathetic noises and customers seemed to like that. She loved it. It made her feel part of the community. She hated the days when Alina made her stay in the back and count endless pills into jars.*

Wolfs Bane, which contained the bitter, poisonous Aconitum in its roots, was used as a herbal remedy by many people in their country, and Alina was often called for help by neighbours who couldn't afford a doctor. Alina made up several teas herself to test the properties so that she could prescribe a safe dosage to those who insisted on continuing to use it. Maarji watched in fascination as Alina weighed different proportions of roots and leaves on the scales, then brewed several variations in carefully labelled test tubes.

The tiny lab room behind the counter was cramped, and the smell from the tea quickly filled ite. The smell dark and woodsy, like a damp forest, with just the faintest bitter note that hinted at the taste. Maarji wrinkled her nose and told Alina she didn't understand anyone who would chose to drink anything that smelled like that when they could just take a pill from a packet with a sip of water.

Alina explained that it took some people longer than others to abandon the old ways for anything new. It was essential to help them, and not to judge them. Maarji thought of the two young men who had staggered into Alina's shop almost doubled up with cramps, perilously close to losing control of their bowels. Even when Alina tried to help them with medicine, they yelled at her and asked for more herbs. Maarji knew better than to argue with Alina, but privately she decided that she definitely judged them.

When Maarji woke in the darkness a little while ago, the smell hit her. For a moment she thought she was dreaming about being in Alina's shop. Hot tears sprung into her eyes as she pictured the way her sister rolled her eyes whenever Maarji spoke. She usually wanted to punch Alina when she made that face, but right now, she would do anything to hear Alina call her ridiculous.

Did Alina even know she was missing, Maarji wondered. They weren't in close touch. They exchanged Christmas cards and the occasional text every few weeks or months. She was fairly confident hadn't been in the darkness for more than a few days. It was a strange notion to consider. She imagined Alina happily going about her business, cycling into the shop each morning and maybe having dinner with friends before she went home. And all the time, her sister was trapped in the darkness and was thinking about drinking poison.

She was not going to drink the poison. She wasn't even considering it. She would rather die from starvation. She would rather die from anything she had chosen herself than give into this tea that had appeared in the darkness.

Aside from anything else, she wouldn't give Alina the satisfaction. The thought brought a tiny smile and the unfamiliar movement made her cheeks feel achy and stiff and itchy. She imagined Alina flying to Sweden to identify her body and being told she had died of Aconitum poisoning. Her lips would tighten, that little pursing thing they did whenever Alina thought that Maarji was an idiot. Maarji knew would try to be dignified and not speak ill of the dead, at least not in front of the Swedish authorities. Sooner or later, though, she wouldn't be able to help herself. She would blurt to someone that she couldn't believe Maarji of all people had been stupid enough to drink the thing she had judged so many others for.

Maarji reached out to touch the cup again. It was already barely lukewarm and a horrible wave of regret rose up in her. She should have drunk it while it was hot. The soothing warmth would have been worth whatever came next.

In sudden anger, Maarji swiped at the cup. She barely had the strength to knock it over, but she heard the faint thud as the china hit the metallic floor. The puddle trickled towards her and she pushed herself back against the wall, her chains clinking.

So it was gone. Would another cup arrive, she wondered? Would she have the strength to resist if it did? Maarji curled herself into a little ball and closed her eyes. She didn't know.

39

'What if it's a different killer?' Johan said, handing me a bowl of porridge the following morning.

'Two killers in this little village?'

'There are five missing women, but only one body found so far. Either the killer intended to move Leyla and was interrupted, or they decided to let her be found.'

I nodded. The porridge was gorgeous. He'd made it with creamy soy milk, nuts, honey and spices. 'Neither of those scenarios is particularly uncommon,' I said. 'Five victims in just a few months suggests someone unravelling, losing control. They could either be getting sloppy, or have a growing need for the world to know what they are doing.'

'Okay, but even so, escalating directly to displaying the next body on the fire for the entire village to see is quite a leap,' he shrugged. 'You said that church is quite remote. Even if people walk by it now and then, the killer has relative privacy in the middle of the forest with which to do whatever they do. Even at night, the clearing next to the village is exposed. There are buildings around it and the possibility for a boat to pass by. It was a huge risk.'

I sipped the last of my coffee as I thought this over. 'I interviewed a forensic psychologist once, who explained that the way a serial killer presents the body — or doesn't — gives away as much about their psychology as who they chose as their victim, sometimes even more. The sheer symbolism of burning someone in such a public way — it makes you think of medieval torture, burning women accused of witchcraft, that sort of thing.'

'What was the English guy you celebrate burned for?'

'Treason. The celebration is that he was stopped. Guy Fawkes tried to blow up the Houses of Lords to kill the king and reinstate a Catholic monarch, but he was betrayed by an anonymous letter.'

'Seems quite an extreme punishment for someone who didn't even succeed in his plan.'

'Medieval criminal justice isn't really known for its measured reasonableness,' I said. 'Are you thinking that Axel was being punished for something?'

'I am thinking there was a different intention behind his death.'

I refilled both of our coffees and crossed my ankles in his lap as we sipped in companionable silence for a moment. 'I wondered about him doing it himself,' I said. 'To evade capture if he thought the police were on to him.'

'Climbing on to the fire alone?'

'It's possibly more likely than someone else managing to carry a dead weight up there without destroying the fire.'

'Did Axel know the police were going to approach him yesterday?'

'Maybe not, but he was questioned about Maarji, and I asked him about whether he knew the family Leyla worked for. Maybe that was enough. I'm going to try to go to his house today,' I announced.

'Ellie —'

'I'll be careful. If Pernilla or any other family are there I'll back off.'

'If they see you there —'

'Then I'll tell them I'm coming to pay my respects. They're the ones who think Axel and I were a lot closer than we were — I might as well use that to my advantage. I can't just sit here —'

'It's not safe.'

'No,' I gave him a rueful grin. 'None of this is.'

I WAS ROOTING AROUND THE BEDROOM FOR THE HOODY I'D discarded sometime the day before, when I heard Johan's phone ring.

'*Hej Linda*,' he said, and my ears perked up.

I went back into the lounge and he put his phone on speaker. I frowned, trying to follow as much of the Swedish as possible. She was explaining that while she had been thrilled to hear from Cissi, the more she thought about it, the more she wasn't sure it sounded like Cissi. The text had included lots of emojis and text speak. Linda's daughter reminded her that Cissi was weirdly snobbish about emojis, insisting that there was nothing wrong with using proper language for messaging.

Also she had remembered that Cissi had an iPhone. The message Linda had sent in response to her text had been delivered in green as a text. It was possible Cissi had got a new phone in the past few months or had been out of wifi service in whatever country she was in, but now Linda just wasn't so sure about anything.

Could someone else have sent a text pretending to be her? she asked Johan in Swedish.

He looked up at me as he tried to gently explain that it was possible.

But why? Why would anyone do that? I just want to know she is safe. Linda's voice dissolved into sobs, and my heart went out to her.

Johan asked if she had forwarded the text or shown her phone to the police, and when she said she hadn't, he suggested it might be a good idea. They may be able to trace the phone it had come from. Linda took a shaky breath and said she would do that as soon as possible.

Then it seemed that Linda's daughter came into the room as there was some muffled discussion in the background.

'Are they discussing the text?' I asked Johan and he shook his head.

'I can't hear all of it, but it's something about Stockholm — I think the daughter ran into Cissi,' he muttered.

'Not Cissi, Tuva,' a voice said in English. 'I was just telling my mother that she shouldn't be so gentle with Tuva. There is something bullshit about her.'

'You saw Tuva in Stockholm?' I asked. 'When, exactly?'

'*Fettisdagen*, last year.'

Fettisdagen was the same day as Pancake Tuesday. Mid-February? I looked at Johan but he was ruffling through his notes with a frown. He minimised the call and searched for something on his phone.

'*Fettisdagen* last year was the day Cissi was due to fly to Hong Kong,' he said.

'Exactly. Tuva wasn't sitting around waiting to say goodbye like a normal person.'

'You're sure it wasn't Cissi you saw?' I asked. 'If she was

flying out of Arlanda, maybe she killed a few hours in Stockholm for some reason. Whereabouts did you see her?'

'It was on Söder and it was Tuva,' Linda's daughter said firmly. 'Cissi is normal and friendly. It wasn't her. I saw Tuva and she is a fucking weirdo.'

40

Tuva Hallström's house had a closed down feel, I thought. I could just about spot her nearest neighbours through the trees. One garden was cheerfully scattered with children's bikes and garden toys, the other house strewn with cosy fairy lights and candles glowing in the windows. Tuva's house looked blank somehow, every window dark and empty. But she must have been home because Johan was inside.

We'd worked out a plan of action on the bus. Tuva would know immediately that the visit was about Cissi if she saw me and might clam up, so we decided that Johan would approach her alone. I'd hang about nearby so that he could ring if it seemed that she would talk to me too. Or if he needed me.

A chilly gust of wind hit me, and I shivered. I'd wandered down to the water's edge, a small rocky beach that ran along the back of Tuva's garden. Nerves fizzed in my stomach and I felt restless, uneasy. I wasn't sure why. The shock of seeing Axel's body was still buzzing around me, I thought, just waiting until I had a moment to process it.

There was nothing to be nervous about today. I had no reason to think Tuva was anything other than a bit socially awkward. And weak heart or not, Johan was a big guy that anyone would think twice about —

What? The worst she would do was toss him out on his ear. He'd already got further than me: she had let him in. Maybe that was what had put me on edge. I'd anticipated hanging about the trees at the edge of her driveway, observing their conversation.

Instead, she had stepped aside and shut the door behind him. I'd hurried round to the back, and just glimpsed her at the kitchen window, presumably pouring coffee. Then she'd moved away and been engulfed in shadows and I hadn't seen a sign of life since.

I sighed and paced the beach a bit more. A glance at my watch confirmed it hadn't even been ten minutes. I looked at my phone. No call or text from him. I could message him, I thought, or even ring him in the guise of checking whether he'd be home for dinner or something. But what was the point in disturbing them? A call might even distract Tuva, prevent her from saying something important. I opened a couple of messaging apps. They all showed Johan last online about half an hour ago, which was when we had got off the bus.

It was the unexpectedness of her inviting him in, I thought. She had been quite firm that there was no chance I was getting over the threshold. I'd taken her for a hermit who would never let an unexpected stranger in. If anything, I would expect someone like that to be more apt to trust a woman than a strange man. Clearly, I'd got her wrong. Maybe she just hadn't liked the look of me.

Little, angry waves rushed against the beach. The sea was choppy but not wild, deep blue and white-tipped. I found a large and flat rock to sit on and hugged my knees close to my chest.

I wouldn't have taken the Tuva I met for random day trips to Stockholm, either, I thought. Something about the whole situation didn't add up. Cissi stayed with Tuva for a few weeks before taking up her new job abroad. Sometime just before she was due to leave, the sisters got into some kind of argument. Cissi left — presumably to catch the flight to Hong Kong that she may or may not have made. And Tuva popped to Stockholm — for a spot of shopping?

I knew she was a freelance accountant. Could she have had a meeting with a client that just so happened to fall on the day her sister left? That was quite reasonable, but Tuva had told me specifically she was at home the morning Cissi was due to fly. You could drive to Stockholm in less than two hours, but Tuva didn't have a car. It was at least three hours by public transport.

A noise from the house caught my attention, and I sat up straighter, but it was just the wind flapping the fabric of a sun lounger. I stared at the impenetrable windows for several minutes but saw no sign of them. A quick glance at my phone confirmed nothing from Johan.

With ants in my pants, I got up and wandered a little farther up the beach. The coast curved around a corner into a tiny, secluded bay with even a couple of patches of sand. Ancient, gnarled trees leaned out over the water, and I couldn't tell if this was still Tuva's property or part of the forest.

It was lovely. The water looked ankle-deep for several metres, and I could just imagine the twins as little girls, splashing about in the shallows and making up stories about the fairies who lived in the intriguingly twisted tree trunks that lined the secret beach. It was just out of sight of the house, and it was easy to pretend it was magical and invisible to adults.

Then I realised that I couldn't see the house anymore. I turned to hurry back to the big flat rock, but something caught my eye. A blue ribbon, tied around a branch, fluttered in the breeze.

'Hey.'

I jumped a mile as Johan appeared behind me.

'What are you doing down here?' he asked.

'Are you okay? How did it go?' I hugged him, relief trickling through me though I was fully aware I was being ridiculous.

'It was weird.'

'Weird, how?'

'I gave her the story you suggested, about how I was a journalist writing a story about Swedish girls who au pair abroad and the dangers they might face. That was when she invited me in, but then she wouldn't talk about Cissi at all. She kept changing the subject, asking me about myself.'

'Asking about you?' I edged closer to the ribbon. It was ragged and faded. I suspected it had once been a deep royal blue but had been weatherbeaten into an uneven greyish blue.

'Yeah, like where I come from and what I like to do. She asked if I had a girlfriend.'

'She was hitting on you?'

He shrugged uncomfortably. 'I don't know.'

'It sounds like it.'

'We did say that the singles scene up here must be rough.'

'Still, she was all judgy about how man-crazy Cissi was, and then she pounces on some random dude who knocks on her door.'

'Yeah, but a pretty good looking random dude,' Johan grinned.

'Sure, sure —' My laughter died on my lips. I ducked under the branch where the ribbon was tied and stepped over a root. Tucked between two thick roots was a little pile of rocks, each smaller than the one below, to form a small tower.

'What is that?' Johan asked.

'I think it's a cairn,' I said quietly. 'A memorial that marks something like a place of death, or it could be a place to remember someone when you don't have a gravestone. I thought it was a Scottish thing, but I suppose there's a lot of crossover between Celtic and Norse traditions.'

'I wonder why she would create a memorial when she insists that Cissi isn't missing.'

I crouched down to examine the cairn a little more closely, and my blood ran cold when I saw the tiny letters carefully painted on the top stones. 'Because it's for Tuva,' I said.

41

Dusk had fallen by the time the bus trundled towards the village. Most of the buildings sat shrouded in darkness, but Pernilla's shop was lit up. I wondered if she was working or if somebody was covering for her. I hadn't dared show my face at the shop yet. Luckily we'd frozen most of my mammoth haul from a few days earlier, but sooner or later, I was going to have to face her.

Johan was leaning against the window, clearly fighting to stay awake. I held his hand, wishing there was a way I could carry him the rest of the way to the cottage. It was only a couple of kilometres, but even I could do without it after the day we'd had.

'So we know now why Cissi did not want the police looking into her disappearance,' Johan murmured sleepily. 'It was too much of a risk they would figure out it was Tuva missing. And why she wouldn't give a DNA sample.'

'I thought identical twins had the same DNA,' I said.

'Not quite.' He yawned and rubbed his forehead in an effort to rouse himself. 'Or at least, not always. Once the zygote splits, mutations can occur as they develop in the womb, leading to variations in DNA.'

'Is that something an individual would be aware of?'

'Only if the mutations had caused visible physical differences, or if they had previously had their DNA investigated, for some medical reason perhaps. Either way, it is a risk she presumably was not willing to take.'

'And none of that does anything to suggest what happened to Tuva,' I added with a sigh.

I thought again of the woman on the boat with Axel. I'd not managed to see Cissi this afternoon. Johan's back had filled the doorway, blocking my view, and I was kicking myself for not warning him beforehand to step aside so I could catch a glimpse.

'So was it Cissi in Stockholm that day, then?' he said. 'Linda's daughter seemed pretty certain it was Tuva.'

I shook my head. 'I think it was,' I said slowly. 'I think that's the key — Tuva is missing, and she was last seen in Stockholm. We should talk to the daughter again, see if she can remember anything else, if she was with someone — and I'll ring Nadja. She's based at the station in Mariatorget — maybe there is something she could do to look into Tuva's movements that day, even off the record.'

'It does seem more and more as though the twins are not related to the other four women,' Johan pointed out. 'They all worked with children, and they were all based far from home — Cissi never fit that bit, and Tuva doesn't fit at all.'

THE BUS PULLED UP OUTSIDE PERNILLA'S SHOP, AND WE GOT off. I glanced across at the café, hoping for a chance of a bit of sustenance before trudging the rest of the way home, but there was no sign of Tariq. I shivered and slipped my hand into Johan's. The village was always quiet, I reminded myself. It just felt eerie tonight.

'We'll go slowly,' I smiled as we started the walk. The clouds were thick overhead, denying us even a scrap of moonlight so that just a few steps past Pernilla's shop, we were plunged into almost complete darkness. We held onto each other as we seemed to take turns tripping over roots and rocks with every second step.

'I am tired,' he admitted, proving his point with a jaw-cracking yawn. 'But I am not —' he hesitated, searching for the word. 'Destroyed. And today has been a lot of activity. I am getting better, Ellie.' He tried to say it casually, but he couldn't keep the hope from his voice.

I reached up and pulled his face down for a snog. We staggered into a rut in the road and half-fell against tree slimy with melting moss because we were sexy like that. 'You were always the best,' I grinned when we came up for air, wiggling my eyebrows to undercut the horrifying cheese.

He sniggered and sang a couple of lines of that Tina Turner song, sounding curiously like the ungodly screech of a mating fox. We were still arguing over which of us was the worst singer between us when headlights appeared on the road ahead. The car crunched over the road, which wasn't intentionally gravel but was so badly maintained it might as well have been, dazzling us with full beams until it pulled up next to us and our slimy tree.

I still had white spots dancing in my vision as the driver's window lowered and Officer Karl smiled at me.

'I've been looking for you, Ellie,' he said.

42

'What the hell is this?' Johan demanded.

I was grateful for his forcefulness because I didn't think I could form a sentence yet. My breath felt tight in my chest. It was as though the air had been sucked out of Karl's cramped office. My eyes scanned over the printed pages again and again, refusing to take it in.

'I think it is clear —' Karl began.

'No, it isn't. Explain, please. Why do you have this? What is it?'

'It appears to be an online diary that Axel kept.'

'Fantasy,' Johan spat.

'Well —' Karl glanced nervously at me.

I wanted to jump in, to shout indignantly, to stand up for myself — but my voice remained trapped in a hard lump in my throat. For an instant, the world wavered in my vision, and I was grateful for Johan's warm hand tightly gripping mine. Just a breath or two. That was all I needed, then I would be able to speak again.

'A sick fantasy. How *dare* you present this to Ellie with no warning, no preparing her — you were going to have her face it alone, without even me for support?'

Karl had tried to make Johan wait in the outer office, but Johan had insisted he came or we waited for a lawyer.

'Ellie isn't underage or otherwise unable to —'

'It's got nothing to do with that, and you know it. It's a question of human decency. Before we leave, I will require your supervisor's name and the best way to get in contact with them. This is unacceptable.'

'Well, I —'

'Ask me what you need to ask me,' I managed finally.

'You don't have to answer anything, Ellie.'

'I know.' I squeezed Johan's hand with a faint smile. 'But this is a murder investigation, and I want to help. If these — things that Axel wrote about me are relevant to what happened to him, or would help find Maarji or any of the other women —' I forced myself to make eye contact with Karl. 'Ask what you need to ask me.'

Karl blinked. He seemed to have no idea where to start.

'If you want to know if I knew about this, then no, I absolutely did not,' I said. 'I won't dignify a query as to whether any of it is true with an answer. If it were —' I shuddered, my voice again swallowed by horror. I forced myself to take a deep breath. 'Then you would be able to see marks on me.' I rolled up my sleeves, worrying, for a horrible, absurd instant, that there would, in fact, be rope and whip marks, but no. It was just my normal arms. 'Clearly, I have nothing to do with any of this, so what do you want to know from me?'

'Are there diaries like that about Inga or Leyla?' Johan asked suddenly.

He was right. The entries Karl allowed us to skim

through concerned me in the church and — I closed my eyes. I couldn't even bring myself to think about it.

I don't judge anyone's sexual proclivities. Whatever consenting adults get up to is entirely their business as far as I am concerned, but that level of pain — I couldn't wrap my head around it being pleasurable. I'm not going to go into any further detail, but to be clear, we're not talking spanking or light bondage. It was dark and violent and filled with hatred. Johan had read a little further than I had been able to, and by the thunderous look on his face, I guessed it didn't get any better.

'This is the only diary.'

'That you have found so far,' I whispered.

'How do you know Axel wrote it?' Johan demanded. 'The username is just numbers.'

The printouts were from an online diary, like a blog, though the domain name appeared to be a random sequence of letters and numbers. None of the standard blog hosts would allow content like this. Years ago, I'd written an article about the dark internet, online communities that met in shadowy, encrypted corners to exchange content much like this. I remember being horrified that the men — because, like it or not, it was always men — who thought this stuff, never mind shared it with strangers, walked amongst us. Sat opposite us on the tube, stood next to us in crowded pubs trying to get the barman's attention. And now I was the subject of one.

'His laptop was signed into the username,' Karl said quietly. 'The laptop has been sent to Stockholm for analysis by data tech and forensics. They have confirmed that the entries were uploaded from the laptop and that fingerprints suggest only Axel used it. If they report more, I will inform you.'

Karl looked baffled and more than a bit overwhelmed. He had clearly jumped to the conclusion that this diary implicated me in some way but was now coming to realise I was a victim. I could practically hear the gears grinding in his head as he tried to keep up.

'You knew Axel well, is this the sort of sick thing he thought about?' Johan demanded and Karl flinched. 'This content is a crime.'

'No, he — I don't know. Axel had a very difficult life —'

'A difficult life?' Johan slammed his hand hard on the desk, making all three of us jump.

Karl's eyes narrowed. 'Is this not the sort of thing a boyfriend would want to avenge?'

Johan burst out laughing, a sharp, angry laugh that didn't sound like him. 'Yes,' he said coldly. 'But I can barely walk up a flight of stairs without getting dizzy. I wish you all the luck in proving I carried a man almost the same size as me onto a bonfire nearly three metres high.'

'What do you mean by a difficult life?' I persisted. 'What happened that was so difficult?'

'He never told you about his sister?'

The woman in the boat, I thought. 'He once mentioned a sister in passing, but I don't know anything about her.'

'She died when they were children.'

'That is awful.'

'Axel and Pernilla — of course they were grieving, but it was like they turned in on themselves, hid away from the world for two, three years. My mother was once close friends with Pernilla, so we would go to visit, but they never answered the door. Mamma brought me so I could shout to Axel, ask him to come and play. Sometimes I saw him watching us from his bedroom window, but he never came down. Then one day, Pernilla opened the shop again and it was as though everything was normal.

They seemed happy, they lived their lives, they almost never mentioned Ulrica. But my mother always said they were never the same again. I've known Axel my whole life,' he burst out suddenly. 'He can be troubled but he would never —'

'How did Ulrica die?' I demanded.

'She —' His eyes widened as he realised what he was saying. 'She ate a poisonous plant.'

43

'We must go to Stockholm immediately,' Johan said. Karl had dropped us off at the cottage, and I built the fire as Johan paced like a caged tiger. 'Get a taxi, it doesn't matter what it costs. We could stay with Maddie and Lena. I can't protect you.'

'I don't need you to, you plonker,' I muttered.

'Ellie —'

'Axel is dead. Even you could fight a dead man.'

'This isn't —'

'No it's not funny,' I sighed. 'But I'm not running away to Stockholm. Not yet. There's something I'm missing.' I stood up as the kindling took alight with a cheery crackle. 'There is something I know — some connection. I need to go to Axel's house.'

'Ellie —'

'I know. It's stupid and dangerous, and if you suggested going I'd do my nut in. But I have to, I'm so sorry.'

'Let me come.'

I shook my head. 'I need to be able to run away.'

He nodded, reluctantly accepting this. 'Promise you will run away the instant you are uncomfortable. If someone is there —'

'I'm not going to barge in and confront Pernilla, I promise. I'll approach carefully and only get anywhere near close if it's definitely empty.'

'How could you be certain —'

'If I know Axel, the whole thing will be glass. I've no doubt a psychologist would have a field day with his open designs and secret every bloody other thing. I will be a giant wuss about it, I promise.' I wrapped my arms around his waist and pulled him as close as I could. 'I have no intention of not coming home to you.'

'I am going to phone Lena,' he said gruffly into my hair.

'That is an excellent idea.'

I kissed him then started the laborious process of getting my outdoor clothes back on. When I was sufficiently layered, I paused by the door.

'Lena is not answering, but I've left messages for her and Maddie,' Johan said. 'I'll keep trying them, but hold on —' He opened his iPad, then my phone buzzed with a Zoom notification. 'I know you might go out of service, but it's recording. I will watch the entire time and if you freeze for too long I will call 112.'

I nodded. 112 would likely route to Karl so be about as much use as an inflatable dartboard, but he needed to do something. It would be nice to have him nearby, albeit in my pocket. I opened the door. I wanted to give him another hug, but I also knew that I wouldn't let go if I did.

After some consideration, I decided to cut through the forest to get to Axel's house, rather than taking the main road through the village. It's interesting how relative fear is, I thought as I tramped into the deep, shadowy woods. At least the moon had come out, so there was a slight silvery glow taking the edge off the darkness. Most of the time I, like any sensible person, would avoid a dark forest at all costs, but compared to where I was heading, the trees felt familiar and safe.

The scariest possible thing in them was a bear or a wolf, I thought with a determined grin. What was a bit of lethal, feral teeth action compared to the horrors humans dished up for one another. I wanted to whisper the thought out loud to Johan, but I was afraid of my voice carrying on the silent night.

I couldn't let myself think about what little I had read in Karl's office. If I let myself remember happily jogging along beside Axel, blethering nonsense as he thought about *that* — I'd never sleep again. The setting of the church chilled my bones. Johan's question about whether there were entries about Bahar, Inga, Leyla, and Maarji was good. The things Axel had written and the fact we knew at least three of them ended up in the same place— I stumbled in the darkness as horror ricocheted through me.

I couldn't let myself go there. Taking a deep breath, I carefully packed all that away for the time being and made a mental note to look into virtual therapy sessions in English. I fumbled in my pocket and pulled out my phone, needing to see Johan's face. He was there, watching intently. He smiled, mouthed *are you okay?* I nodded, though I knew all he could see of me was a silhouette.

'I'm nearly there,' I whispered. My voice sounded crashingly loud in the silence. Where was the howl of the wind when I needed it? I strained my ears and realised that I could hear the water lapping gently against rocks somewhere nearby. 'I've passed the church, and I'm heading downhill again. His house is on the water, so I think if I follow the coastline I'll hit it fairly soon.' I glanced down and realised that the soft forest floor had given way to slickly wet rocks. Even with the faint moonlight, I couldn't see the sea, but it couldn't have been more than a couple of metres away. I stepped forward gingerly.

'I can see you on *Find my Friends*,' Johan said softly. 'You are right at the water's edge.'

I was actually standing in a few centimetres of water, I realised. By the light of my phone I could see white foam rushing around the little rocks beneath my feet before being drawn back into the sea. I walked on, even more carefully. It would be bloody morning before I got to Axel's house at this rate. I gave Johan a quick smile and he whispered that he was here and I stuck my phone back in my pocket. I couldn't look at it and concentrate on my footing simultaneously.

While water didn't hold quite the same dread for me that it once had, I still wasn't much of a swimmer. Of all the ways I could die tonight, bumbling into the Baltic Sea and drowning would have to be the stupidest. The thought brought a snigger and I felt ever so slightly more myself.

The trees stopped quite abruptly at the edge of a lawn. Whether my eyes had adjusted or there was a bit more moonlight, I wasn't sure, but I could clearly see Axel's house. And it wasn't even close to what I would have predicted. It was a neat cottage, bigger than ours, but not much, in traditional Swedish clapboard style. The paint finish was impeccable despite the harsh winter we'd just had. It put me in mind of something I couldn't quite grasp.

The garden was carefully tended, with sprigs of daffodils

and tulips dotted around the borders. Hanging baskets on the porch burst with colour, and as I made my way along the edge of the lawn towards the house, I could smell a thriving herb garden. Mint and dill grew like weeds in the Swedish climate, but I knew Axel was a gardener of epic proportions when I caught a whiff of basil.

I paused by a large rhododendron bush and pulled out my phone, turning the camera outwards to give it a sweep around the house and garden. I wasn't sure how much it could pick up in the dark, but it was worth a try. Johan must have been able to see something as he raised an eyebrow.

'I thought it would be like the library,' he said.

'Yeah.'

I would definitely have pictured Axel in some sleek space-agey affair. This was the home of a kindly elderly couple who pruned roses in companionable silence on summer's nights, and fell asleep on the porch buried beneath the Sunday papers. This was a house to bake bread in.

The front door slammed and it was a miracle I swallowed my scream. My heart thudded as a powerful engine roared to life in the driveway, headlights silhouetting the house.

'Ellie, stay there —' Johan hissed, but I was already running.

Clutching my phone in my hand I stole, as lightly as I could, around the side of the house. Keeping to the shadows, I crouched and peered around the corner. I couldn't see anything other than the bonnet of the car without leaning far enough out to risk being spotted. As I heard footsteps crunch across the gravel I held my phone out, ensuring that just the corner where the camera was stuck out from the side of the house. Doors slammed then the car took off with a spray of gravel.

'Did you see anything?' I asked.

'It was Pernilla,' Johan said. 'Karl picked her up. She had an overnight bag with her.'

44

Johan hated this. He hated everything about it. He hated that Ellie was out there in the dark, in danger. He hated that it was entirely right and sensible she had said he shouldn't come with her.

His hands were clasped together so tightly that his shoulders ached as he bent over the iPad. The brake lights of Karl's car had long since disappeared, and Ellie had slipped around to the back porch. He could only see an awkward angle of her shoulder as she held her phone in one hand and tried the door handle with the other.

'Thought nobody locked their doors out here,' she murmured as it rattled uselessly.

'Try the top of the door frame,' he said quietly. Even though they had seen Pernilla leaving, they couldn't be certain that the house was now empty. He heard a ping and Ellie's muffled annoyance as she felt around the deck for the fallen key.

'Nice one,' she whispered, holding the key up to the camera. 'Not just a pretty face, are you?'

Stop making jokes and concentrate, Ellie.

He knew that humour was her way of coping. One day in Thailand, she had told him the story of how the undertaker at her gran's funeral had taken a wrong turning and ended up heading up a very narrow one way street in the hearse. Ellie and her mum, in a taxi behind, had been in absolute hysterics watching the coffin reverse back towards them, pursued by a furious London cyclist in a weird full-body lycra suit. He'd been red-faced with the exertion of thumping the bonnet of the hearse, then shook a random fist at the taxi for good measure before cycling off, which had set Ellie and her mum off again. They'd ended up scandalising the congregation by giggling all the way through the funeral. Her sense of humour was one of the many things that made Johan realise his life wasn't worth living without Ellie in it, but now he just wanted her entire focus to be on staying safe.

Actually, he wanted her to be on the sofa next to him, and for the sofa to ideally be in Stockholm. The screen had gone black again; she must have put the phone back in her pocket as she carefully inserted the key in the lock. He heard the faint click and her gasp of triumph and his heart sank as he realised the door was opening. The next thing he heard was the creak of a floorboard. Blood pounded in his ears — was that Ellie's footstep or someone else's?

'That was me,' she whispered, and he let go of a shaky breath with a soft chuckle. There was no point in telling her to be careful, but he was about to anyway when there was a thud at the front door. The sharp knock came again, so hard that the thin door rattled.

'Who the hell is that?' hissed Ellie.

'I'm not answering it. I'm staying with you.'

Another knock, louder and more urgent.

'You need to answer it,' she hissed. 'I'm in the hallway, near the back door. I'll stay here while you do.'

Johan still hated tearing his eyes from her even for a second, but he reluctantly darted to the door and opened it. Five teenagers in requisite black crowded on the front step, looking furtive. Johan gave them an impatient stare.

'What do you want,' he barked in Swedish. 'I'm busy, I don't have time —'

'Is the English lady here?'

'No.'

'We need to talk to her. When will she be back?' The spokesperson was a tall girl, poker-straight blonde hair streaming out from beneath her black woollen hat.

'What do you need to talk to her about?'

They exchanged unsure looks and Johan sighed. 'If it's important, you need to tell me.'

'It's about the church,' the tall girl said.

'Come in.'

There weren't nearly enough seats in the cottage for five extra people, so two sat cross-legged on the floor, two at the kitchen table and one in the weirdly lumpy armchair next to Ellie's writing desk. Johan glanced at the iPad screen as he sat back down on the sofa, but it was black. Why would Ellie put her phone back in her pocket while she was waiting?

'Wait,' he said to the kids. 'Ellie?'

'I'm here,' she whispered. 'The moon is gone so it's even darker. I'm sure there's nobody in the house.'

'Stay there anyway, please,' he said. 'You should hear this too.' He looked up at at the kids. 'Something about the church?'

'Should we speak English?' the tall girl asked.

'If you don't mind,' Johan replied. 'Ellie can hear.'

He could see that sparked curious glances, but he wouldn't elaborate further. 'So?'

'My uncle said she wanted to speak to us about when we were partying at the church,' the tall girl said.

'When were you partying at the church, exactly?'

'October,' she replied promptly. 'We wanted to do an authentic Halloween celebration and séance, and the area around that church has the thinnest veil between this world and the next for many kilometres around.'

She looked so earnest that Johan kept his expression impassive. 'Okay.'

'We were extremely respectful of the space and left it exactly as it was we found it. We had every right to spend time in our own community church.'

'Of course. What did you want to tell Ellie?'

'My uncle said the English lady wanted to know if we saw anything unusual when we were there.'

'And did you?' Johan bit down the urge to snap at her to spit it out.

'We saw a woman. Just twice, both times she was leaving the church as we were arriving. I didn't think anything of it at the time, I didn't see her very clearly and she didn't leave behind any sign she had been doing anything other than exploring. But as the English lady asked —'

'Did any of you recognise the woman? Have you seen her around the village or anything?'

They all solemnly shook their heads.

'Do you know Pernilla who runs the shop next to the ferry dock?'

Repeated head shakes, a couple of shrugs.

'She's an older lady, blonde hair, maybe 175cm or so —'

'Yes, that sounds like her. She was old,' the tall girl nodded eagerly.

Johan glanced at his iPad but the screen remained stubbornly blank. He hoped Ellie was catching it all.

'What age, roughly?' he asked.

'About your age.'

FURTHER QUESTIONING HADN'T REALLY CLARIFIED WHETHER the woman they saw was younger than Pernilla or they just thought he and Pernilla were the same age, Johan reflected as he closed the door behind the teenagers a few moments later.

'What do you think, Ellie,' he asked as he picked his iPad up. She didn't respond. With growing horror, he realised that it had gone to sleep. 'Ellie?' It would only do that if the call was disconnected. He opened the screen, tapping urgently on the Zoom app, but only his own image stared back at him. 'Ellie!'

45

I ran.

I had been crouching awkwardly on the hardwood hallway floor, listening to the teenagers debating whether Johan was younger than any of their parents, when I realised I could smell something. It took me a moment to place it, but familiarity, quickly followed by horror, washed over me.

My gran had been a keen gardener and I'd spent many a contented afternoon after school round hers, obediently weeding and sewing and pruning under strict instructions. Her rose garden, a selection of stunning bushes that lined the back wall of her postage-stamp-sized garden, was the pride of South London, according to her. I privately thought the Chelsea Garden Show might have something to say about that, but I kept quiet as Gran barked orders at me to clip them in an exact way to ensure that they bushed and flourished just as she wanted.

And that was what I could smell now. Not roses; it wasn't the scent of flowers but of freshly cut stems. Stuffing my phone back in my pocket, I slipped into the kitchen and my stomach heaved as the smell got stronger. Forgetting myself for an instant, I automatically fumbled on the wall for a light switch, then jumped as I remembered and slammed the light back off. But in the flash of illumination, I'd spotted the deep lilac, bell-shaped flowers, pointy leaves and stringy, light green roots. Little posies were strung along the back wall to dry.

A bitter odour hung around an enormous heavy, pestle-and-mortar on the wooden counter. I saw that dried leaves had been ground up, then put into small cheesecloth bags, which were lined up in neat rows on the scrubbed pine table. I counted ten in the top row, ten in the second — and nine in the third.

I sprinted out the back door and down the driveway towards the village. They were taking a bag of tea somewhere. That meant one of the victims was still alive. *Maarji.* It had to be. I had to find her.

My lungs burned painfully and my legs were already starting to tremble, but I kept going. Afraid of getting lost in the dark, I avoided the forest, racing down Axel's long drive to the main road. The lights of Pernilla's shop beckoned in the darkness, I caught movement in Tariq's café out the corner of my eye as I belted past. The impeccable barn on the outskirts of the village. The one I'd joked to Johan must contain pallets of cocaine. It was the same style and absurd standard as Axel's house. It was a long shot, but my gut propelled me on.

There was no sign of Karl's car near the barn when I finally reached the clearing. I couldn't decide if it was a good sign or a bad one. My breath came in choking, gulping gasps as I started to move around the outside of the barn, searching for a door.

I finally found a door at what felt like the back of the barn, facing the field. It was small, just a standard doorway as far as I could make out. Wasn't the whole point of barn doors to drive tractors and fork lifts in and out? There was, however, no handle. My heart thudding, I rammed it with my shoulder the way I've seen in movies. Shockingly enough, it didn't give.

'Maarji!' I yelled. My voice sounded thin and reedy and no match for the solid, ungiving door. 'Maarji, I am here to help you! Are you in there?'

Silence throbbed back at me. I tried kicking the door, succeeding only in jarring my knee like nobody's business. I looked around wildly, desperately hoping for some tool, some weapon conveniently lying in the woods that I could use to batter at the door. Could I run back to the village for help?

I kicked the door again, then a muffled snuffling startled me. I looked round to see the Best Dog in the World, Official, pawing urgently at the walls of the bard, whining mournfully. I had never been so happy to see another living creature in all my days.

'Hiya, mate,' I whispered, and he whined in response. 'You can smell something in there, can you?'

My stomach twisted as he pawed again, his nose pressed in a tiny gap between the slats. I hadn't noticed the gap. I crouched down and gently shouldered him out the way, tapping my phone's flashlight on with trembling fingers.

With my face pressed up to the gap, I got a faint scent of what had the dog so excited. It was foul, a sort of sickly sweet, rancid odour that put me in mind ever so slightly of — oh god. My stomach heaved, and I clamped my hand over my mouth. A butcher's shop. Gritting my teeth, I grabbed my phone from the grass, took a deep breath and shone it into the gap.

The scream tore from my throat before I even registered what I was seeing.

46

Blue lights filled the darkness as several ambulances and police cars parked haphazardly around the clearing. Several police officers had offered to let me sit in their cars and get warm, but I shook my head every time. I couldn't move.

Sheer self-preservation had sent me staggering backwards when I spotted the first skull. I'd sprawled on a thick tuft of grass in the field a few metres back. The dog had come to sit by my side, so close he was practically on my lap as I dialled 112 with shaking hands. It had routed to a call centre in Väddö, and the kind operator had stayed on the line, talking calmly as the world span around me, until the first blue lights appeared.

I'd called and texted Johan several times, but the calls had gone straight to voicemail, and he hadn't seen the texts. Those bloody teenagers must be keeping him chatting, I thought dully as I watched the now all-too-familiar crime scene tent being erected around the barn door. The dog shuffled his comforting bulk even closer.

'Hi, Ellie.' A man squatted near me. Medium-height with

sandy hair and brown eyes, his thick all-weather jacket hung open to reveal a well-ironed shirt and neatly tied tie.

'Are you Lena's friend from Norrtälje?'

'Andreas, yes.'

I nodded. I knew I should probably shake his hand, but my arms were wrapped around the dog's warm, broad back. I didn't think I could let go.

'Firstly, I must thank you.' His voice was soothing. *He should do one of those meditation podcasts,* I thought. 'This discovery you have made tonight will bring closure and peace to the families of these women. I apologise that my team and I did not work quite fast enough to spare you. May I ask how you knew Axel Pettersson owned this barn?'

'I didn't. It was a wild guess, really. It looks like his house.' I shrugged. 'I know that doesn't really make sense.'

'I hope to hear the details of all you have been doing very soon. Please know that we are grateful for your help. I think my team could use a mind like yours.'

'Are they all there?' With great effort, I gestured vaguely towards the barn. A bright flash lit up the barn as officers meticulously photographed every millimetre. I flinched and the dog leaned his massive head on my shoulder.

Andreas hesitated. 'It will be some days before we can make formal identifications, and there is confidentiality until the families are informed — but I think you deserve what information I can give you. One wears a gold chain with an Arabic letter around her neck —'

'Bahar,' I murmured.

'— and another has a tattoo that matches the description given to us by Inga's family. There are also some older remains that will take much longer to identify.'

'What about Maarji? She's been missing less than two weeks.'

He shook his head.

'Then she could be alive.'

'Yes. And we are —'

I scrabbled to my feet, wavering with the sudden effort of being upright. Andreas grabbed my arm to steady me. The dog got to his feet and growled softly at Andreas, as though warning him that I was his responsibility.

'They left with the tea barely an hour ago. She could be drinking it right now. We need to find her.'

'Ellie, I must ask you very strongly to —'

'No offence, Andreas, but you can't order me to do a damned thing.'

47

'My son would never hurt anyone,' Pernilla whispered.

She clutched that strange little bag she had been carrying since they left Axel's house, twisting it and turning it over in her hands. Karl kept his eyes on the road. The temperature had dropped sharply, and he was afraid of hitting black ice. The last thing he needed right now was to crash.

'All those women, Pernilla,' he said softly.

'He wanted them to love him. He deserves love like everyone else. It was just that they didn't understand what a precious soul he is.'

She was talking about Axel in the present tense, Karl realised. His hands were clammy on the steering wheel.

'What did he do, Pernilla?'

Her only answer was a sharp intake of breath. She squeezed that damned herb bag again and the smell in the car sharpened. Karl took the next exit, slowing to a halt at the red light at the end of the slip road.

'If those women had just taken a moment to see the real

Axel — none of it would have happened. None of it was necessary. They were stupid, selfish — he just wanted to be happy. Everyone deserves happiness; everyone deserves love. They should have given him a chance.'

'Those things he wrote in the diary —'

'So what?' she spat. 'All men have imaginations. If that English slut hadn't led him on, he never would have thought those things.'

'They weren't nice things, Pernilla —'

'It doesn't matter now. He's gone. Both my babies are gone.' She twisted the bag so hard that it broke open, and the foul-smelling leaves spilt over her lap. 'How can a mother live with that?'

'Where are the women now, Pernilla?' Karl asked. 'If you tell the police, help them give the families peace, they might be a little easier on you.'

'Why should I give any family peace? I have no peace. I just want to be with my babies.'

She picked up the tiny dried leaves, put a pinch on her tongue and swallowed. Horror filled Karl's chest as he realised what they were.

'Pernilla, no —'

He reached out and tried to swat her hand away from her mouth, but it was too late. She licked her hands, swallowing more and more of the leaves as the car swerved alarmingly, skidding on the frosty verge as they reached the outskirts of Norrtälje.

'I will just be with my babies,' Pernilla whispered with satisfaction. 'The tingling is beginning already. It's easier this way.' A cold smile spread across her lips. 'It's always easier this way.'

'Just a few more minutes, Pernilla, please —'

Karl put his foot down and sped through a red light,

praying the junction was clear. He thought of that first day she opened the shop again after Ulrica died. His mother had run to her and tried to hug her, but Pernilla pushed her away, waved her off as though she were an irritating bug. All smiles.

Pernilla, how are you? Did you take those pills from the doctor? Please come over when you close the shop, have dinner with us, you and Axel. You're not alone —

Isn't it a beautiful day? Spring is on the way.

A horn honked angrily, but they made it through and he spied the police station up ahead. His mother's worried eyes, the way she squeezed his hand as they left the shop. *We must let them grieve however they see best. We will just let them be, for now, and then —*

He turned sharply and slammed the brakes on as relief washed over him. He leapt from the car and screamed for help. Just a few more moments, and it wouldn't be his problem anymore.

Uniformed police officers were already appearing at the door as he yanked open the passenger door. Pernilla tumbled into his arms.

'Pernilla, please — just tell me one thing — who killed Axel?'

She chuckled, her voice thickening as her tongue started to swell. Foam appeared at the corners of her mouth as her breathing became laboured.

'That's easy,' she slurred as her eyes started to flutter closed. 'It was Ulrica.'

48

Adrenaline coursed through me as I ran the couple of kilometres back to the village. His house? I hadn't even searched any further than the kitchen. Had she been there the whole time?

Black spots danced at the edge of my vision, and the world took on a trippy, surreal air. I slowed to a jog, forcing myself to breathe deeply. I had to hold it together.

The dog trotted along by my heels. The lights of Pernilla's shop danced wildly as I tripped over my own feet, held onto my knees for support. I felt for my phone and realised it wasn't in my pocket — Andreas. *Shit.* I'd dropped it when I staggered and he grabbed it, then I didn't give him a chance to give it back.

'Ellie?' Tariq flung open the door of his café, his hands covered in flour. 'What is happening? Do you need help?'

'I need to find — I don't know where to —'

'Breathe, slowly.' He took my arm and I leaned gratefully against him.

'I'm fine, honestly — Maarji, the other missing woman, she could be alive —'

'Why don't you come and take some coffee, get some strength before you —'

The dog barked sharply, echoing in the still night. I hadn't even noticed him leaving my side, but he was over by the library.

The library.

Axel's library. With a fresh burst of energy, I ran for the door with Tariq just behind me. Of course, it was shut for the night, but I jiggled the handle anyway. The small town cliché of no one locking doors finally worked in my favour, and the door swung open,

'Wait here a moment, I'm coming with you,' Tariq said firmly.

He ran off. I stood, obediently frozen with my hand on the handle. The library awned before me, silent and brooding, tall bookcases silhouetted against the windows. The dog whined, turning himself in surprisingly agile circles and figures of eight.

Tariq returned with a powerful flashlight, Kadin in tow clutching a crowbar.

'There are no armed robbers in this village,' Tariq smiled, nodding to the crowbar. 'But better to be prepared.'

'There must be a basement or a cellar,' I said, leading the way through the silent shadows. 'He couldn't risk someone hearing her scream.'

I felt the look that Tariq and Kadin exchanged behind my back, and I was grateful that they didn't abruptly turn and march right back out of there. I wouldn't have blamed them.

At the back of the public area, there were three doors. The first led to a storeroom piled high with books and papers. The second was a toilet. The third door was locked. I pressed my ear to it, but I couldn't hear anything.

'Stand back,' Kadin said quietly.

Tariq, the dog and I obeyed and watched solemnly as he battered the handle off with the crowbar, then produced pliers from his pocket, which he used to drag the bolt back from inside the lock cavity. The door swung open, revealing a long, dark staircase.

'Let me go ahead,' I said, slipping past the two men. 'If she is down there, it might be easier for her to see a woman first.'

Despite my words, my legs very much did not want to venture down the steps. Luckily the dog helped out by tramping ahead, lolloping down the stairs in his lopsided way. Clutching the bannister for support, I followed.

The stairs led to what appeared to be a standard basement. By the light of Tariq's flashlight, we could see a large, state-of-the-art boiler/heating system thing, several cardboard boxes, some of which had books piled on top. The space was filled with that gorgeous new book smell, and for a moment, I was afraid I had got it completely wrong.

'It is much bigger,' Tariq said quietly.

I looked around and saw he was right. The library was around the size of a large classroom, equal to maybe two or three normal sized-rooms. Tariq walked a few steps forward, shining his light all around. The initial open area where we were standing was roughly the same size as the library. Tariq's flashlight revealed multiple corridors leading off the main area before fading into complete darkness. A vast, intricate maze spread beneath and beyond the village. I wondered if one of the corridors would even stretch as far as the barn.

Kadin was standing at the foot of the stairs, holding his crowbar rightly, his eyes wide and terrified. I went to him and gently prised the crowbar from his grip. He blinked at me.

'Do you know the barn at the edge of the field a couple of kilometres that way?' I asked.

'At the foot of the left boob,' he muttered, and I nodded.

'Go there. There are hundreds of police. See if you can find a detective called Andreas, but if not, tell any of them what we've found. We need help. It would take us hours to search this whole place, and Maarji might not have that long.'

He nodded and scuttled gratefully up the stairs.

Tariq turned to me. 'Do we wait, or —?'

'We make a start. It might be pointless, but —'

That was when I heard the faint tapping.

49

Voices. People's voices. Real ones, not even in her own head, echoing around the metallic walls.

Maarji wanted to cry with relief. They were going to find her. They had to. What else would they be doing down here?

There was a woman's voice, but it wasn't Her. She sounded completely different. She sounded — like TV, Maarji thought vaguely. Maarji's mind was so wooly and confused that she thought she was dreaming again.

Why did the woman sound like TV? Then she realised — she was speaking English. She was talking like those dramas Maarji loved, where people had long dresses and parasols and stared judgementally at one another over cups of tea.

What was somebody English doing in Maarji's prison? It didn't make any sense, but she didn't care. It wasn't Her, and that was all that mattered.

Then the voices faded. They were moving farther away. They didn't know she was here!

No, no, no, she murmured. She was so weak. She couldn't remember the last time any food had appeared in the darkness, *and her stomach ached. But she couldn't let them leave. She had to let them know, somehow.*

She felt around in the darkness until her fingers touched cool china. There were so many cups, most of which she had flung or shoved out of reach so that she wouldn't be tempted by the warmth, but this one, she could touch. She had to reach further than her arm wanted to go before her fingertips curled around the handle, just enough to drag it a tiny bit closer.

Concentrating every final scrap of energy she had left in her, Maarji wrapped her fingers around the handle, lifted and banged it down on the floor. It made a metallic ting that reverberated around her skull. Was that loud enough? She didn't know — but it had to be. Gritting her teeth, she lifted the cup and banged it again, and again —

50

'Here — it's coming from in here —'

We'd reached the end of the third corridor we tried. Each one had several thick, metallic doors leading off them. We'd listened at each, torn between urgency and fear of missing the next faint, metallic ping.

Horror curdled in my guts as I counted just how many doors there were and thought of Andreas's words. *There are also some older remains that will take much longer to identify.* How many?

This was the door. The dog agreed. He whined and pawed urgently, staring at me as if to ask why on earth I wasn't just opening the door.

'Maarji!' I yelled. 'We're here to help you. Hang on — it won't be long now.'

I heard a muffled moan in response. I whacked the lock with the crowbar, but it just bounced back off. 'Help is coming Maarji — we're going to get you out!'

Footsteps thundered down the stairs, then Kadin appeared with three uniformed police officers and two paramedics in tow. One of them carried what looked like a very delicate chainsaw.

Relief flooded through me as the officers ordered us to stand back. As a high, metallic drone filled the air, the dog gave short, sharp barks, straining against his collar. It felt like forever as the officer worked with precise urgency until finally the door sprang open, and there she was.

'SHE WILL BE OKAY,' TARIQ SAID FOR THE HUNDREDTH TIME.

The three of us huddled together, watching as Maarji was loaded into an ambulance, an oxygen mask secured firmly over her face. A curious crowd had gathered, a handful of the Café Ladies, one or two of the Bonfire Men. *What had we been walking above all this time*, I thought.

Maarji's eyes had flared in terror as the emergency workers burst into the tiny room, a bit like a bank vault, where she had been held. She fainted as the paramedics reached her, but one of them reassured us that her pulse was steady as they gently lifted her onto the stretcher.

'She is very strong,' she said with a brief smile.

Looking around at the spilt teas puddling around her prison, I could see that was true.

'Yeah, I think she will be,' I said now, forcing a smile.

'I'm going to get coffees for the workers,' Tariq added. 'Ellie, please come and eat and drink something —'

'I need to get to Johan,' I said. 'He's been waiting on me all this time. I don't even know what time it is, my phone —' I sighed, remembering. 'I should get it from Andreas first —'

The crowd of villagers had grown, and a few stepped up to help Tariq as he brought out trays of baked treats that had been prepared for the following day. The smell of coffee nearly brought me to my knees, but Johan was my first priority.

As I turned to leave, something occurred to me. 'Kadin, do you know the family Leyla worked for?'

He nodded. 'I was not introduced to them, but I saw them from a distance once or twice.'

'Have you seen them recently? They're not here in the crowd, are they?'

'No, definitely not. They went back to Stockholm the day after Leyla's body was discovered. I guess they did not want to answer questions about Leyla's employment status in Sweden.'

The kitchen. The butter. The book on the sofa.

'They've been in Stockholm all this time?'

'Yes. I went up to speak with them when I heard of Leyla's death, hoping we could remember her together. But they were packing to leave. The father ordered me off their property, and then I saw them drive away.'

The kitchen. The butter. The book on the sofa.
And something else.
The clothes.

Then I realised, and it all fell into place.

51

'Andreas!' Lena shouted into the phone.

She was driving with one hand on the steering wheel as she sped up the E18, significantly breaking the speed limit, cursing the fact that this car didn't have a siren. At least traffic was light, she thought as she undertook a Volvo going barely 100kmph in the fast lane. She was only just passing Täby. There was at least an hour to go, even at this speed. *Shit.*

'*Var är Ellie? Är du med Ellie?*' she barked, wanting to scream when Andreas said that Ellie was gone.

'My colleagues are with her, but I stayed at the crime scene for the moment —'

'Are you in touch with any of them? Speak to them now — make sure they can see her.'

'What's going on? What do I tell her?' Andreas asked. Lena could hear that he was running, and she appreciated he didn't waste time questioning her.

'Tell her —' Lena closed her eyes, remembering the meeting she had been called into less than an hour ago. She swerved around a long lorry laden with logs and pressed her foot further down on the gas. The speedometer nudged above 170, headed for 180. 'The results came back from Linda Hallström's DNA sample. The cousin of Cissi and Tuva. There was a match in the system.'

'Ellie has found the victims that match the DNA samples in the church,' Andreas said in surprise. 'There is no sign of Cissi Hallström here.'

'I know,' said Lena. 'She was never there. Cissi Hallström is alive and well as far as we know, but Tuva Hallström —'

'I'm at the village — Ellie left a few moments ago, going home to Johan —'

'Follow her. Now. Tuva Hallström was one of Mia's followers. She went into that water that night — with Mia, instead of Mia, we don't know for certain. They bear a strong physical resemblance to one another.'

'Wait, what? What are you are saying —'

'Linda's DNA matches that of the remains we identified as Mia. Mia may be alive. And if she is alive, Ellie is not safe.'

52

'Hello, Ellie. Long time no see!'

Mia didn't look any different. For some reason, that was the maddest thing for a moment. In my imagination, she'd grown into a grotesque, powerful gargoyle, with palpable evil rolling off her in waves. But sitting at our kitchen table with Johan, she looked just like Mia.

Just as she'd looked that day in the boat with Axel.

'Close the door, Ellie, you're letting a draught in! Johan, has she not got used to living in Sweden yet? Warmth first, Ellie! Always!'

The fire huge, logs stuffed the stove right to the chimney. They were blazing furiously, flames licking the glass. The angry crackle filled the cottage.

She'd lit the candles on the table. We always joked about how we meant to get around to a candlelit dinner, but our dinner didn't seem fancy enough to warrant it whenever we thought of lighting the candles. The table was heaving with a variety of dishes. Johan's plate was piled high.

Johan sat facing me. Mia had pushed her chair back a

little to twist around to greet me. He was conscious, he didn't appear to be tied up or in pain. He didn't tear his gaze from Mia as she leaned over to pat the chair next to her.

'Come and join us! You are welcome, Ellie. You always were. I wish you had known that.'

'Thank you,' some bizarre manner-reflex inside me muttered. I hesitated, my mind whirring as I tried desperately to think of a plan. I was still right by the front door. I could fling it open and run — but what would she do to Johan?

Had she already done something to Johan? I stared anxiously, trying to catch his eye. He was so quiet.

'Please, Ellie,' Mia said, a note of sharpness in her voice twisting my guts. 'Don't hang about by the door, it makes me uneasy.'

'Well, we wouldn't want that.' I crossed the lounge and sat where she indicated. I didn't see that I had any choice.

I could see the dishes clearly now and recognised them as almost everything that had been in our freezer. Mia dished up for me, piling random spoonfuls of pasta and curry and stew onto my plate. They were all sprinkled liberally with dark, dried flecks. No prizes for guessing what they were.

'*Äta upp, Johan,*' she singsonged, then slammed her hand on the table, making us both jump. '*Smacka gott!*'

A moan rose in my throat as he took a bite of creamy pasta and chewed carefully. Mia's eyes narrowed as she watched. His eyes filled suddenly with tears and he went into a coughing fit, doubling over as his chest rattled. He fumbled for a napkin and covered his mouth.

'You're not swallowing any of it,' Mia screamed.

He wiped his mouth as his breathing gradually settled. Sweat had broken out on hs forehead.

'A choking sensation is common with heart disease, Mia,' he said quietly.

She frowned, her head cocking a little to one side like a demented dog. I missed the dog. I wished I could have brought him home with me, but his owners showed up looking for him just as I was leaving.

'I would love to know the results of your last EKG,' she said, her eyes lighting up. 'When did you last get an echo?'

'The structure of my heart is surprisingly intact.' He shuffled food around his plate with his fork, quite impressively giving the impression he was eating without actually lifting the fork to his lips. I recognised the technique as one he used to avoid my cooking.

'Mia, what is the plan here?' I blurted. I couldn't handle a diversion into geeky medical chat.

Mia took a mouthful and cringed. 'Ellie did you make this? It's terrible.' Her food was also covered in the black specs. 'I tried to warn Axel you weren't exactly perfect, but he would never listen.'

'The whole *way to a man's stomach* thing is pretty old fashioned now.'

'Yes, I suppose so. But at least Johan is a good cook; Axel was as bad as you. It would never have worked. He should have listened to me. It was pathetic.'

'Is that why you killed him?' I asked, trying to match her dinner-party-conversation tone.

She shrugged, wrinkling her nose as if to say *sort of*. 'He lied. I hate people who lie. I never lied, Ellie, did you notice that? If you had just asked me what happened to Sanna or Gustav or any of them in all those months, I would have told you. But you never did. I really thought we could be friends, but you never trusted me. Johan's girlfriend's never liked me. I hate it when women don't trust other women, don't you?'

'Yeah, it sucks,' I said, trying to copy Johan's shuffling food technique. The problem was, I was ravenous. My stomach growled at the thought of wolfing the whole plate down. I thought of Maarji, resisting the teas for days and days.

'What did he lie about?' asked Johan.

Mia rolled her eyes. 'Johan, you would have been furious. You get so protective. The fire was for you. It was what you would have done if you could. Do you wear a device that checks your blood saturation levels? I would love to know —'

'You killed Axel because of his diary,' I said. 'You found it online somewhere?'

'I have been very lonely and bored these past months, Ellie. Online friends are better than nothing.'

'But you were already here in the village for days before he died. You were staying at the fancy house on the hill.'

She nodded, taking another large bite. She chewed for a few moments before replying. I saw Johan slip a few forkfuls off his plate onto the floor. I was closer to Mia, so I didn't think I could do so without her noticing, but she didn't seem bothered about whether or not I was eating.

'That was lucky,' she said, swallowing finally. 'I was going to find an empty summer cottage, but they are so unpleasant without fire and then someone notices the smoke — I have had to move on so many times, it is quite exhausting. But I was exploring a little and the stupid family left a back door unlocked, so it was a charming base while I got to know Axel and his interesting mother.

'I was going to kill you,' she announced, swivelling suddenly towards me with a bright smile.

I gritted my teeth to return it. I was shivery and my teeth were on edge. Darkness shimmered at the edge of my vision.

I reached for the basket of crusty bread, realising that the leaves hadn't stuck very well to the crusts. I managed to tear a relatively leaf-free chunk and nearly cried with the joy of swallowing something.

'I thought you were cheating on Johan,' she added with a *silly me* grin. 'Then I met Axel and figured out that he was just fantasising. He thought you were his type but not really. He needed women he had a chance of breaking, who would be so grateful that he rescued them from days of darkness that they would be willing to play his ridiculous games in the church.' She giggled and sipped her wine. 'The poor idiot didn't understand why they died as soon as they arrived at the church. He thought it was the spirits of the gods or something. It was his mother, of course, saving him from becoming a murderer. Parents are extraordinary people. Äta, Johan!'

In sudden irritation, she flung her glass of red at him. He didn't flinch as the purple liquid dripped down his face. It was then that I noticed the two syringes laid neatly next to her plate. She followed my gaze and smiled.

'Second time lucky,' she trilled. 'Whatever unpleasantness the leaves bring, don't worry too much, it won't last long. I'm sorry, Ellie, but I think you must go first. It feels right. Sanna, Liv, you. One, two, three! Poor Johan, anyone would think I was secretly in love with him.

'I'm not,' she added, turning to him.

'I know,' he said. Sweat trickled down his brow and it seemed to be an effort for him to stay upright. He must have swallowed more of the leaves than he meant to. Aconitine wasn't that potent; she must have laced them with something. 'You love Krister.'

Mia flinched. 'Anyway, that's the story of Axel —'

'Krister still loved you,' Johan said firmly.

Mia flinched again and stared at her plate. I could feel his words bore into her.

'Even with everything that he knew about you. He would never have stopped loving you. You know Krister. His loyalty was more compelling than any rational thought. He should have dumped me as a friend a long time ago, but he never did. And he never would have left you. He would have come with you, if only you'd let him.' Johan's voice was soft, mesmerising, powered by a cold fury that chilled me.

'But you killed him.'

'No —'

'He followed you into the water that night, and you let him. You cared more about escaping than you did about him. You let him down. You killed him.'

'It was an accident —' she whispered.

Krister's Hammarby top. It read *Nacka*, his favourite player on one side, and *Krister* on the other. Johan had won it for him in some raffle twenty-odd years ago. It was what I'd seen in the pile by the breakfast bar in the fancy house. I'd seen it and not registered it properly, just like I'd seen Mia and twisted the flicker of recognition into something else.

In my defence, she did look a little bit like the Hallström sisters.

'You don't have accidents, Mia. You could have saved him. Instead you saved yourself. If you really wanted him to be alive, then he would be.'

'No. Nooo —' Her voice dissolved into a soft moan, fingers curled around the syringe. I tensed, ready to smash her face in if she made a move.

'He knew, at the last moment. He died knowing you didn't care about him —'

'NOO —' she screamed.

She grabbed the syringe and swung for him -- I yanked

the back of her chair out, dumping her on the floor — she struggled but I was on top of her, straddling her —

Johan dropped to his knees and pinned her wrist to the floor.

She thrashed wildly, scratching my arms, my face, with her free hand as I flailed to hold her still.

'*Fucking* keep at peace,' I roared, sinking my teeth into her hand as her scream filled the cottage.

We knocked into the table, sending crusty bread and lasagne toppling over us —

And the other syringe. She lunged for it with super-human strength as a deafening smash sounded and the glass on the wood stove shattered —

A burning log rolled onto the mat which started to smoke instantly —

Mia grabbed the second synge and plunged it in Johan's direction as I held her arm back with all my might. I bit her wrist as savagely as I could but she seemed impervious to the pain —

'Johan, get back —'

The needle hovered centimetres from his shoulder, but he was oblivious as he focused on getting the first from her other hand —

'JOHAN!' I screamed as the door burst open and a team of uniformed officers stamped through the flames to us.

53

The day of Krister's memorial dawned bright, flooding Nytorget with startling sunshine. A selection of hipster sunbathers looked on awkwardly as Krister's family, colleagues and friends from school crowded around the little square, holding hands, clutching photos of him. The fountain sparkled, and the sky was a flawless deep blue, stretching endlessly above beautiful Stockholmers sipping coffee, riding old fashioned bikes with large wicker baskets, chasing after designer-clad toddlers.

Johan was going to speak in a moment, but now Krister's father was addressing the crowd. A tall man with kind eyes, he spoke warmly of his son, raising a few laughs as he remembered Krister's unending tenacity when it came to proving he was right. Tears filled Johan's eyes, but he smiled down at me, gripping my hand firmly.

'Are you okay?' I asked softly. He kissed the top of my head.

We were flanked on either side by Maddie and Lena. Maddie held my other hand, and I knew that Lena held Johan's arm. *We weren't alone*, I thought. I closed my eyes briefly, remembering Krister's sardonic grin, his unwavering loyalty to Johan, the way he loved to torture me by driving his speedboat like a maniac.

Mia's trial was scheduled for the following week, but that was barely a dot on our consciousness. The prosecutor had assured us she had evidence coming out the eyeballs. We might not even need to testify.

Johan's flat had sold within a week. I was stunned but was reliably informed that was standard practice for Söder. We signed the final paperwork for our cottage in Nacka that morning. It offered the country peace we had got used to but was a twenty-minute bus ride from the city. I glanced at my watch. My mum's plane would be landing any minute, and I was already braced for the lectures I was about to get regarding our lack of packing progress.

Johan was starting classes on Monday to renew his nursing license, so he needed to be within commuting distance of the city's hospitals. Also on Monday, I had a final interview as the Nordic correspondent for an international news website. I'd worked for the editor before, on a manky free paper in Camden, and I knew she liked me. I was pretty sure I was a shoo-in.

And that was us. No fairy-tale glitter or dreams come true. Nothing special or even particularly interesting. Just life. Johan and me and the people we loved.

Happy ever after.

THE END.

THANK YOU

That's all from Ellie and Johan — for now! If you have enjoyed the trilogy, you might enjoy some of my other books. Have a browse at FIKABOOKS.COM

and use code STOCKHOLMMURDERS to get 15% off your first order as a wee thank you!

Claire xx

ALSO BY CS DUFFY

The Dark of Night Series

The Shadow City Series

This is Not a Romance

Printed in Dunstable, United Kingdom